THE BILLIONAIRE'S CHARADE

JEANNETTE WINTERS

Jeannette Winters
Author Contact

website:
JeannetteWinters.com
email:
authorjeannettewinters@gmail.com
Facebook:
Author Jeannette Winters
Twitter:
JWintersAuthor
Newsletter Signup:
www.jeannettewinters.com/newsletter

Also follow me on:
BookBub:
bookbub.com/authors/jeannette-winters
Goodreads:
https://www.goodreads.com/author/show/
13514560.Jeannette_Winters
Pinterest:
https://www.pinterest.com/authorjw/boards/

DEDICATION

This book is dedicated to my friend and reader, Koreen. It might have been my stories that brought us together, but your friendship surpassing anything I could ever write. Thank you for always cheering me on and sharing my stories with your friends.

And also thank you to my editor Taryn Lawson, and to Jade Webb at https://meetcutecreative.com/ for another amazing cover!

And to my readers. You continue to challenge me and I love it. Please keep those emails coming!

THE BILLIONAIRE'S CHARADE

Dylan Lawson will do whatever it takes to keep Lawson Steel on the top. The lies and secrets from the past threaten crumble it all. He wasn't about to let anyone ruin what they had worked so hard to build.

Sofia Marciano had a dream, and she wasn't living it. It was within her grasp. All it was going to take was some quick thinking and finding a way to live two lives. She wasn't going to sit back and let her dream slip through her fingers.

When her family starts to question things, a very sexy stranger steps up, and comes to her rescue. Dylan was the perfect cover. No one would ever suspect what she was really doing in New York with him by her side. It was beginning to look like she really could have it all.

Their attraction is powerful and their simple charade becomes very complicated. Is this yet another set of lies, or is their love the one thing that survives through it all?

Sofia walked out of the back room mumbling while carrying the tray of pasta high above her head. This was far from ideal, but what choice did she have? She had only one hour to prepare and she wasn't about to blow it just because she was supposed to be working. She also couldn't risk being over-heard. Her parents would flip out if they suspected what she was up to.

The one nice thing about working for your parents was, she didn't need to worry about getting fired. The downside was what they expected from you. Since her brother Sal wasn't interested in continuing on the family name, either by giving them a grandchild or running the business, it seemed both fell to Sofia. She could sit down with her parents a million times and they wouldn't hear her. They wanted what they wanted, and one of their children was going to make it happen. Sofia seemed to have drawn the short straw and was stuck.

It wasn't that Sofia wasn't good at it; she could do this job with her eyes closed. Heck, she had the same finesse with the customers as her mother, and her skills in the kitchen weren't too shabby, either. None of that changed a thing. She wasn't her mother, and the last thing Sofia wanted was to be tied down to the restaurant. Up early and to bed late. Never really going anywhere or seeing anything. Sofia had dreams, big dreams. She wanted the bright lights, the luxurious lifestyle, the cameras flashing and people calling out her name.

They call my name all the time here, when they want a refill or the check.

"Sofia, table four is waiting for their pasta puttanesca," her mother shouted from the kitchen.

"Yes mama," she replied as she continued weaving through the tables. It figured the time that she needed to get out of work early, was also the night they seemed to be extra busy. Of course, her mother had to put a sign out front saying, "Buy one entrée, get one free." She tried containing her frustration, but it wasn't easy.

Raising the tray even higher, she swayed when she should've swerved when one of the patrons spilt wine on himself and stood up quickly. It triggered a chain of events that seemed never-ending. His chair flipped and knocked the back of Sofia's knee, she grabbed hold of another person's shirt and she could hear the fabric ripping. Letting go, she tumbled to the floor, her tray went in the opposite direction. Shrieks and swears could be overheard, but barely. It was her mother's voice that seemed to echo through the room.

As she struggled to get back up on her feet, her mother was apologizing to everyone. At one point, she would've sworn she heard her mother call her clumsy. Instead of standing there arguing, she began cleaning up the mess with one of the dish washers. Her father came out from the back, took her by her elbow, and led her into the kitchen.

"Sofia, go home," he said.

"Papa, I can't. Mama needs me." Home sounded great, but wasn't where she wanted or needed to be.

He reached up and pulled some spaghetti out of her hair. "And you, my dear daughter, need a shower. So do some of the customers. Now go before your mama comes in here and gives us both an earful."

At times like this, being daddy's little girl worked in her favor. She placed a kiss on his cheek and said, "Thank you Papa. I'll see you tomorrow."

"And your mama too. So best sleep well tonight."

Sofia nodded and walked over to grab her purse. She held it extra close to her as she slipped out the back door. It wasn't that she was concerned anyone would rob her, but there were important papers in there she didn't want to fall out.

Once she was inside her Jeep Liberty, she opened it to confirm all was safe and sound. Pulling out the papers, she looked them over. "Thank God." Sofia tossed them on the passenger seat and pulled away. It was unfortunate that it had all gone down this way, but really, it was perfect. She was getting what she wanted without having to ask. Because if she did, she'd have to lie, and that wasn't something Sofia felt comfortable doing.

Good thing I'm a pretty good actress.

There wasn't much time to waste. She took the fastest shower and put on her makeup so she could be back out the door. It wouldn't matter if she knew the lines or not, if she wasn't there on time. Thankfully, the traffic lights were in her favor and before she knew it, Sofia found a parking spot and was entering the theater house.

Her heart was beating fast, as though she were about to take the stage in front of an audience. There were hundreds of people trying out for the role. It wasn't even a lead part, either. Sofia knew the one thing they all had in common: *We all want it.*

The butterflies in her stomach were threatening to take flight as she took center stage. It was just an audition and only six people, who she wasn't even sure were paying close attention, were the ones she should be concerned about. Taking a deep breath, she cleared her mind and focused on the lines she'd been rehearsing to herself earlier.

If she hadn't been, it was possible she never would've lost control of the tray and...*I'd still be stuck at work instead of where I want to be.*

Sofia knew it was a rough start, but after a few words, the rest of the lines seemed to flow easily. When it was over, someone said 'thank you' and called the next person onto the stage. All she could do was take a seat and wait to see if she was going to be one of the lucky ones. Watching the others, she felt deflated; they all seemed good. Sofia didn't have a portfolio to set her apart from the others. All she had was a passion, which she'd yet to reveal to the world. Was this going to be her break? In a few minutes, she was going to get the answer.

Her cell phone vibrated and she looked at the caller ID. It was her mother. One call that she should take, but no way in hell was she answering it in the theater. With the acoustics, she was positive her mother's voice would be heard by all, and even in Italian, they would get the point: Sofia was in trouble.

Declining the call, she turned off her phone and slipped it back into her purse. There would be hell to pay for this tomorrow, but tonight, she just wanted one shot at her dream.

"Number seventy-one," the stage manager called out.

That was her. What was going on? She got up and headed right over.

"I'm Sofia. I'm number seventy-one."

He handed her a bag and said, "Please put this on."

Taking the bag, she looked inside. It was filled with torn and tattered clothing. "I'm sorry, I don't understand."

"You are going to the second level. Read the instructions, we will be monitoring you outside."

He left her alone and she pulled out the paper.

YOU ARE A PAUPER. A BEGGER. YOU MUST CONVINCE FIVE PEOPLE TO GIVE YOU MONEY IN ONE HOUR. YOU DO, AND THE ROLE IS YOURS.

Never had she heard of such a thing for an audition. It had to be a joke. But as she looked around, there were a few others being handed bags of their own. Sofia wasn't about to question it any further. She wanted this, and if begging on the street was what got her the role, so be it.

She went into the dressing room and quickly donned her new attire. When she looked in the mirror, she realized the clothes were only one piece of the puzzle; she really needed to look the part if she wanted the part. Wiping the makeup off, then tussling her hair, she pulled out hair spray and made it look as though she'd spent the night sleeping on the sidewalk.

Her heart ached as she looked in the mirror again. This was now the face of people she and her parents tried to help. Each night when the restaurant closed, they took all the left-overs and handed them out to the homeless. Nothing was discarded without first contemplating if it could be utilized by someone who needed it. She was blessed to have come from a family who didn't know such hard times, and fortunate that her parents passed down their generous heart to her and Sal.

Pulling from the depths of her soul, she went out the back and into the alley. There was a large cardboard box, and she knew that wasn't placed by any tech crew to set the stage.

Someone literally had spent the night in there. Sofia felt like such a fraud doing this and wanted to turn and head right back inside and tell them no role was worth this. But she reminded herself that if she really made it big like she wanted to someday, then hopefully she could use that money to help more people in need.

Turning away, she took all she'd seen firsthand and prepared to use it now. Once on the street, she could feel the looks from people passing by. The men who once would check her out and devour her with their eyes, now avoided making any eye contact with her at all. This might be one of the most valuable lessons she'd ever learned: what it was like to walk in someone else's shoes.

Sofia had no idea who was there watching her and the others, or what the others' roles were. Did it matter? Not really. This was something she needed to do. Putting out her hand, she went up to one passerby.

"Can you spare a dollar?" Sofia asked. He brushed her hand away and kept moving. Her voice had been soft, but he had seen her, just ignored her. Pulling herself together, she knew she needed to beg as though she'd be hungry again tonight if she had no food. In a louder voice, she asked another person. "Excuse me, I'm hungry. Do you have any change so I can buy something to eat?"

"Get a job," a woman in a business suit snapped.

Ouch. Sofia knew some of the people her parents helped had jobs, and lost them. They had homes and lost them. It wasn't the lack of desire to work, it was no work. They were caught in the system. No one would hire them because they didn't have transportation or a place to live. And they didn't have a place to live or a car because they had no job. They couldn't even get assistance from the government with a check because of their homeless status.

6

Of course, she knew not all homeless people were like that, but until you spoke to them, heard their story, how could one judge? Sometimes things spiral out of control and you're left with…*nothing but hope.*

There was a little girl, about six years old, blond braids on both sides of her head. She tugged on Sofia's torn plaid shirt. She didn't say a word but opened her hand and showed Sofia it was filled with coins.

"Wow. Is that yours?" Sofia asked softly. The little girl nodded then put her hand closer to Sofia's. "You want to give this to me?" The girl nodded again. Sofia reluctantly took the little girl's money. Her eyes welled up as she said, "Thank you so much." She fought the urge to pull the girl into her arms and give her a huge hug for having such a kind, sweet heart. Then she noticed the little girl was wearing two hearing aids, and the braids probably were meant to conceal them.

It was so touching that she was surprised she could keep her emotions in line. Sofia dropped to her knees so they were eye to eye. Sofia knew sign language because her cousin was deaf. She brought her fingers to her lips, then brought them forward and smiled. The little girl beamed and signed back, 'you're welcome.' Then she turned and dashed back to her mother, leaving Sofia kneeling on the sidewalk as they disappeared in the crowd.

She didn't know when the sobbing started, probably when she looked again at the coins she held in her hand. Sofia wished she could rush home and share this beautiful moment with her parents. But this was hers alone to carry.

Clutching the coins close to her, she tried to get up off the sidewalk. A quarter fell, then a nickel. With her vision blurred by salty tears, she struggled to retrieve them without her fingers getting stomped on by the numerous pedestrians. As she reached for the last coin, her hand encountered a pair of black leather shoes pointing her direction. A large hand reached down and retrieved the nickel.

Sofia looked up and was about to tell him that belonged to her. Before she could, he said in a deep but soft voice, "I believe you dropped this."

The sun had set and the streetlights above him were bright, almost halo-like around him. How she wished she could make out his features, see who it was behind such a tender tone. Still rocked by her sobbing, Sofia reached up and took the coin from him. She choked out, "Thank you, sir."

As she tried to get up again, she felt a hand on her elbow guiding her up until she was steady on her feet. With her burst of tears, she now realized her contacts had made their escape along with the change. *Damn it.* She couldn't see anything close by without them. But it didn't matter. She'd already decided this little test the theater had created for her was done. The part wasn't worth the emotional turmoil she was in.

Turning, she headed for the wall of the building, which she knew wasn't far behind her.

"Please wait," he called out. "You have options. Let me help." He took her hand and she felt him slip money to her. "My cell phone is on the card. Call me at any time."

She didn't bother trying to read what it said, since it would all look like ant footprints to her. Sofia nodded and gripped the paper firmly as she felt her way along the wall. Once she had come to the corner, it was about fifty steps to the backstage entrance. Whoever was supposed to be watching over her hopefully would be there to let her back inside.

Sure enough, the door opened, and the stage manager said, "You didn't get five, but we are impressed. You were so authentic in your performance that you had some of the others in tears. Brava, my dear. You have the part."

Sofia should correct him. That tearful display wasn't for show. It wasn't for a part. Her heart and soul had been out there for all to see, and they thought they'd been looking at an actress. *You will be so disappointed when you realize I could never fake what you just witnessed, and I wouldn't want to.*

"Rehearsal starts next week. Every night at eight. Miss one and you're out. Do you understand?"

"Yes. What would you like me to do with this?" she asked, holding out the money so he could see her bounty.

"It is yours. Do as you wish." He walked away, leaving her standing there.

Thankfully, she wasn't far from the dressing room, and she knew she had a spare set of contacts inside.

Her night might not have gone anything like she had planned, but somehow fate seemed to have intervened, and maybe things had happened the way they were supposed to.

Now if only my mother could understand that.

"You're not yourself tonight Dylan. What's on your mind?" Gareth asked.

He hadn't been able to stop thinking of the woman on the street since he'd seen her. It wasn't as though he hadn't come across someone begging before. Actually, he and his brothers were very active in the community and supported some of the local homeless shelters. Yet there was something…familiar about her. He couldn't put his finger on it and it was driving him crazy.

"I met a woman today," Dylan said.

Gareth laughed. "That explains the distant look on your

face. Why the hell are you here with me when you obviously want to be with her?"

Dylan shook his head. "It's not like that."

"It never is. So what's her name?"

He shrugged. "I don't know."

"Okay. Names aren't really that important anyway. How about...what does she look like?" Gareth teased.

Dylan couldn't actually describe much about her. It was as though he'd fixated on her, yet the only thing he recalled was her brown eyes. They were filled with...hurt, and he wanted to help. "It's not like that at all, Gareth. She was a beggar on the street and I—"

"Don't tell me you gave her money. What if she is using it for booze or drugs now?"

"She's not that kind of person, Gareth," Dylan snapped.

Gareth snorted. "And you know this how?" Dylan had no answer. His gut telling him sure as hell wasn't going to cut it, not that it mattered. He didn't need anyone's opinion. Gareth continued, "I hate to say it Dylan, but you don't have a great track record with picking the right women."

"I guess that's what we have in common," Dylan said snidely.

Gareth raised his hands. "You don't see me with the hots for some lady hustling for money on the streets."

"No. You find them in expensive restaurants taking you for a lot more."

"Damn. I'd like to argue with you there, but—"

"Yeah. I thought so. But I'm telling you, this woman is different. I...know her. I'm not sure from where, but there's something about her."

Gareth nodded. "We have toured a lot of the homeless shelters over the past few months. Maybe she was there at one of them."

It was the logical answer, but Dylan didn't think that was it. "I gave her my business card. I told her to call me."

"What are you going to do? Give her a job? You don't even know what her skills are?"

It was her connection with the little girl that had gotten to him. It's why he'd reached out and handed her five-hundred bucks from his wallet. Hell, if he'd had more, he'd have turned it over to her.

"I'm not even sure she'll call." But he hoped she would.

"Do you want my help finding her?" Gareth offered.

Although he believed Gareth could help, he also didn't want anyone stepping in to do what he could, or should, do himself. "No. If I want to talk to her, I'll find her myself." He might not have the connections his brother did, but he was resourceful.

"You know how to find me if you change your mind. In the meantime, I wanted to talk to you about Dad."

"Is there something wrong?" Dylan asked. He hadn't seen his father in a few months. Not that he hadn't had time, but he had been trying to avoid the family stuff. He loved them all, but when their father was around, things became…awkward. There was something there that their father didn't want to talk about, and as they got older, it was becoming more obvious. Dylan wasn't one who could sit back and let things develop at their own pace. He liked to make things happen. That didn't always work out so well for him and trying it with their father…probably wasn't a wise choice.

"He's been acting…strange."

"That's nothing unusual, Gareth." Their father might be brilliant in business, but his social skills were lacking.

"I mean, he's talking about Grandfather more and more."

"Yeah. Dad's getting older. That's what old people do. They reminisce. Wait, there will be old photo albums popping

11

out any time now. When they do, just remember who warned you." Gareth got quiet, and that wasn't like him. What did he know that he wasn't sharing? So Dylan asked, "It's not Dad you're worried about, is it? It's—"

"Granddad."

"Gareth, he's been gone a long time. Whatever you want to know now isn't important."

"And if it is?"

Dylan cocked a brow. "Then I hope you'd trust me enough to tell me."

Gareth shook his head. "I don't have any facts to go on, and it's pissing me off. The one person who has been able to come up with anything, doesn't seem to want to help me either."

"Never seen that stop you before."

"She's involved with the Henderson family."

Dylan probably knew more about them than his brothers did. He'd crossed paths with Dean a few times when they were younger. Dean, like himself, had distanced himself from his family at an early age. Although their reasons were different, they ran in the same wild circles for a time.

"Do you want me to reach out and see what I can find out?" Dylan asked.

Gareth chuckled. "You don't even know what I'm looking for."

"No. But if you want my help, then you'll need to share it with me."

"I'm not ready to go to the Hendersons yet. But I'd like you to come with me to see Dad. I have some questions for him, and I'd like you to be there when he answers them."

"What exactly are you looking for, Gareth?"

"Information on Granddad."

That made no sense to him. Dad wasn't a huge talker, and

from what he recalled, which wasn't much, their Granddad was even less of one. "What do you think he's going to say that we don't already know?"

"I hope he knows why Granddad was such an—"

"Ass?" Dylan hated referring to family in such a way, but he called a spade, a spade. Everyone thought he'd never noticed all the shit going down, that he was too young to have picked up on it, but that wasn't the case. Dylan recalled their Granddad yelling at their father on more than one occasion. "Does Charles know you're looking into this?" Not that they needed his approval, but Charles was the oldest and had spent more time with their Granddad. He'd probably be more forthcoming, too.

"I'd rather keep him out of this for now," Gareth said.

"Great. What you really mean is, Charles said leave it alone, and you decided to drag me down with you." It wouldn't be the first time he and Gareth went against Charles's orders.

"Something like that. What do you say? Take a trip with me down south to see Dad?"

"What the hell. Someone's got to keep you out of trouble. When do you want to leave?"

"A couple of days. I'm waiting on some more information."

"Do I need to know?"

"Eventually. We can talk about it on the flight down," Gareth said. "For now, let's just keep this between the two of us."

That was going to be easy, because really, Dylan had no more information than he did when they'd first met. Gareth was good about keeping his mouth shut when he wanted to. This was one of the times Dylan wished he'd run it.

"Fine with me, for now. Can't make any promises later."

Whatever Gareth was looking for had to be big enough that he needed time to confirm. Since Dylan had his own distraction right now, he'd cut Gareth some slack. That wasn't going to last long.

He didn't normally go by that theater, but he was going to again on his way home. With any luck he'd see that mystery woman again. He really hoped she wasn't sleeping behind that building tonight. There was only one way to confirm that. Check for himself.

Getting up from the table, he said, "I got go. I've got a few things to take care of tonight."

"Let me guess—"

"Don't," Dylan barked.

Gareth grinned at him. "I guess I should be grateful you even showed up to meet me."

Dylan replied, "No. I'm a man of my word. And you can count on this, I'll go with you to see Dad, but I'm not saying I'll keep my mouth shut about what we learn. If I think we all need to know, I'll speak up."

The last thing this family needed was to start mistrusting each other. They were in a good place right now, and he wasn't going to let Gareth or anyone else fuck it up over something that didn't mean anything anymore.

"You won't have to. I'll do it first."

Dylan left the bar, pleased with Gareth's response. Hopefully he was pleased with whatever they found out as well.

When he got to the theater, he found the alleyway vacant. He asked around if anyone had seen her, and no one had. There wasn't even any proof that she'd been there. Was it because she didn't want to be found? *Maybe that's a good thing. I don't need anyone who needs taking care of. I'm not that guy.*

Not now, and not ever.

14

2

"I can't believe you did that," Charlene said. "If your parents find out they'll—"

"They won't. Not unless you tell them. No one knows," Sofia whispered. She couldn't believe she was even taking the risk and telling her best friend. Although she and Charlene had known each other since childhood, there was always a chance her mama could get it out of her. Mama had a way of knowing things, even when it was impossible. *Just don't let her find out about this.*

"Well, since she is still upset about your little dinner episode, you might get lucky," Charlene teased.

"And you know this how?" Sofia asked.

"Because I went there for breakfast and when I asked about you, I swore there was a scowl on her face."

"It wasn't my fault. Some guy knocked me over," Sofia defended.

"I think it was your disappearing act that followed that has her perturbed."

Should it surprise her that her father failed to mention he

sent her home? Not really. If her mother was upset, her father would do like any wise soul, and duck and cover. Her mother was the sweetest, most loving and generous person, until she was mad. Then…well it was good she spewed it all in Italian, otherwise some people might be shocked.

"I'm sure it will be okay, since I'm going in early today to cover someone else's shift."

Charlene laughed. "Yeah so instead of eight hours of being in earshot, you now will be there twelve. Good luck with that."

With a heavy sigh, Sofia grumbled, "Why did I call you?"

"Because only a best friend wouldn't sugar coat it. Hey don't worry. It's going to be so busy today, neither of you are going to have time to do anything but work."

"It's Tuesday. It's our slow day."

"Not today. Guess after you left someone booked a large dinner party. Get ready. It's going to be a *long* day."

Overly busy right now was a good thing. "Mama didn't happen to mention who they were, did she?"

"All she said was friends of Sal's."

Her brother had a lot of friends. It came with being a cop in New York. He seemed to know just about everyone. "Is Sal going to be there?"

"Hey, there is your silver lining. He's not. And your mama was saying that she hadn't seen him in almost two weeks. If things start to get heated, just bring up his name."

"Charlene, you're horrible. I thought you liked my brother?" *Sometimes a bit too much.* A lot of Sofia's friends had a crush on Sal, but Charlene never really seemed to get over hers. But Sal wasn't the settle-down type of guy, and she didn't want any of her friends, definitely not her best friend, hooking up with him.

"I was over that years ago," Charlene said, not convincingly at all.

"Good. But I can't throw him under the bus. I might need him. How am I going to explain to my parents that I can't work the night shift any longer? The rehearsals are going to be at seven. Charlene, I can't pass this up, but mama is going to be so…disappointed." Pissed was more like it.

"Emily, the girl you're covering for, might be interested in switching."

"Why?"

"She needs money and let's be real, the tips are better at night. If you're really that good of an actress, then you'll think of a way to sell her on it. And if you can't, then maybe the restaurant is going to be your life after all."

The hell it is. "Thanks Charlene. You're a genius."

"Yeah. I know. You can pay me with a piece of your mama's cheesecake later."

"I thought you were there earlier?" Sofia asked.

"I was."

"And you didn't have any then?"

Charlene laughed. "Don't judge me. It's delicious."

Sofia rolled her eyes. How was it fair that Charlene could eat cheesecake for breakfast and still be so damn thin? Sofia swore she gained a pound just carrying the dishes to the customers. But if she was going to be working full time and also going to rehearsal each night, she was sure she'd be burning plenty of calories.

Too bad I'm a stress eater.

"The only way you're getting that cheesecake is if you come by the restaurant tonight for it. Besides, I'd like to see you in person. This talking on the phone gets old quick."

"Okay, I'll come by. It'd be more fun if Sal was going to be there," Charlene joked.

17

"Don't you think I have enough going on right now? The last thing I need is my big brother asking questions too."

"Sofia, you worry too much. You're a grown woman, not a child anymore. It's time you stood your ground and spoke up about what you want."

"That's easy for you to say. Your parents are free spirits who wouldn't care if you decided you were going to be a tree instead of a human. Mine have mapped out everything. I'm just surprised they haven't planned a wedding yet."

"You're dating someone?" Charlene asked in surprise.

"No. But do you think that would stop my mother?"

Laughing, Charlene said, "Don't forget that I'm your maid of honor."

With a huff, Sofia declared, "There's no wedding."

"And whose fault is that?"

"Don't you start too. You of all people should understand that a woman doesn't have to be married. Besides, I'm only twenty-six."

"Funny, that's the same age I am, and yet I wouldn't mind snagging myself some tall, dark, handsome…"

"Don't you dare say my brother's name. He's not your type," Sofia warned firmly.

Charlene snickered. "Sofia, the problem with Sal is he's everyone's type."

Sofia had to agree with Charlene there. The women seemed to flock to her brother. What was it with that? Did he get all the looks and charm? She might not want to be married, but she wouldn't mind the guys knocking her door down wanting to take her out.

"Although I'm enjoying our little chat, I'd better head to work."

"You already work too much. Now with the show, when do you expect us to see each other?"

"We can talk every day on my way to rehearsal." At one point, she and Charlene had been practically joined at the hip. Now they struggled to find time to squeeze in a night out.

"Before you know it, we'll be just texting each other and then…nothing," Charlene said in an overly dramatic tone.

"Oh please. Who's the actress now?" Sofia said sarcastically.

"Maybe I will need to try out for a part just so we can see each other. Or better yet, why don't you and I go to this event they are having on Saturday night?"

Right now, she was free, and it would be amazing to get out for something fun. "Great. What do you have planned for us?"

"It's speed dating with a paint-a-puppy event after. What can be better? Hot guys and cute puppies?"

"I am *not* going to a speed-dating thing. No way," Sofia said firmly. Her friend should know better than to ask. Sofia was great in crowds because she was a waitress, but speed dating was worse than the real thing. Talk about awkwardly staring across the table at someone and feeling like she had a sign on her, 'I'm desperate.' With the snickering she heard over the phone, it was possible Charlene had been joking anyway. "Seriously Charlene, I need to go in to work now."

"Don't forget my—"

"Cheesecake. Goodness, is that all you think about? Men and food?"

Charlene laughed wickedly. "Sometimes I combine the two. You should try it sometime. Messy but, well, delicious."

Sofia's mind wondered briefly what she could do with some chocolate sauce, but she'd need a partner for that to happen. With this even crazier schedule, dating, never mind a serious relationship, wasn't happening. The last thing she needed was to enter work looking flush from thinking some

JEANNETTE WINTERS

erotic thoughts. Of course, maybe if her mother thought she was sick, she'd go easy on her today.

"I'll have a piece set aside for you. See you tonight." Sofia ended the call before Charlene could try talking her into going. She really wanted to see Charlene and tonight was going to be it.

As she turned and looked towards the entrance, she noticed there were more people lingering around than she had expected. Sofia really should've called her from home instead. She hoped no one accidently heard her. Time would tell.

Instead of going in the front door like she normally did, she tried to sneak in the back and go through the kitchen. Her father was hustling around as usual. She walked over and he leaned back, stopping long enough for her to kiss him on the cheek.

"You're here early," he said.

"Emily needed someone to cover her shift."

"Ah. That's my girl. Always watching out for the restaurant."

He was being so sweet, and that only made her feel more guilty. "Where is Mama?"

"In the dining room. She is preparing for the dinner party tonight. Awe, that's right, you don't know about that yet."

Not everything, she thought. "Who is coming?"

"Sal's friends. They have been here before. Do you remember the Lawson family?"

"Charlie and his wife Rosslyn?"

"Yes, but it is the entire clan tonight. All of Charlie's brothers are coming too. They had come once before for a lunch meeting."

"See all the fun I miss by not working days?" Sofia said

20

laying out the groundwork for when she approached them to switch shifts.

"I am glad you feel that way. Your mama has something she wants to talk to you about."

Sofia was afraid of that. There was no avoiding the chewing out that was about to commence. But the one thing she knew, her mama wouldn't do it where the customers could hear. So, she forced a smile and said, "Then I'll find her now. And don't forget to stir the gravy."

She heard her papa grumble as she left the kitchen. He easily got distracted and no way was she letting it burn on account of her. Sure enough, when she entered the dining room her mother was setting up the table in the far corner. *No better time than the present.*

"Hi Mama. Papa said you wanted to talk to me."

"Yes. We have an issue."

And it is with me. "I'm sorry." She figured she might as well get that out of the way. Why wait until she heard everything she already knew?

"It was about to happen. Change is inevitable."

"Very true Mama." But she knew her mother didn't handle change well. For a recipe, yes, in life, no. "But I'm willing to help out as much as I can."

Mama turned to her and smiled. "You will?"

She'd probably spoken too soon. Sofia wanted to make her mother happy, but not at the expense of her own happiness. "Mama, I said as much as I can. That's all I can do."

Her mother slumped in a seat. "Oh, what am I going to do? I can't lose her. She is the best waitress I have besides you?"

Sofia blinked and tried to see what she had missed. Obviously, the fact that they weren't speaking about her. She didn't want to judge anyone else, but she knew her mother was talking about Emily. "Did she tell you what's going on?"

"Her husband's company switched shifts on him without notice. He was forced to take it or lose his job. Since they can't afford daycare, she now has to switch to working nights. That means I need you here with me to open up and do all the prep, breakfast, and lunch customers. I know this is short notice, but we have no choice. We can't lose Emily and she can't afford not to have this income either."

This was unbelievable. Was it possible that all her worries were for nothing? She was going to be able to have it all, work the restaurant and chase her dreams? It was almost too good to be true, but her mother wasn't one to joke about such things.

Sofia reached out and placed a hand on her mother's shoulder. "Don't worry Mama. I've been hoping to take the morning shift too. This works out perfectly."

"You wanted the morning shift? Why?"

"Because I miss out on so much by working every night." It was the truth.

Her mother smiled. "Ah. I understand. When do we get to meet him?"

Him? Oh God. Her mother thinks this is about a man? Well it was better than the truth. "Someday Mama."

Her mother turned back to setting up the table and was singing to herself. There was no sign of her distressed mood from earlier. Everything seemed to be falling into place. Luck? Fate? Who knew? She was just glad that tonight was going to be a lot better than she'd imagined. If anything, things were looking up, not just for her, but for Emily as well.

As she picked up the silverware and started to help, one thought came to mind. *Maybe the speed dating isn't such a silly idea.*

. . .

Saying no wasn't an option when Charles called a meeting. As one of the owners of Lawson Steel, Dylan didn't want to miss a beat on what was going on. But when he learned the location for the gathering and that Charles was bringing his wife Rosslyn, he no longer felt as though there was an issue. Rosslyn looked like an overblown balloon, waiting to pop. Charles sure as hell wouldn't expose her to any undue stress.

That also meant any family member not showing up for this dinner might want to plan their funeral. His brother was on edge 24/7. It if wasn't bad enough being CEO of Lawson Steel, he was doing everything he could to help Rosslyn with her newly acquired company, Grayson Corp. Dylan was a gambling man, but never would've bet Charles would be so intimately linked to the competition.

He may not have liked Maxwell Grayson, but Dylan had wanted him in prison, not dead. He wasn't sure if Charles ever disclosed what they had planned for Maxwell. If Rosslyn did know, she didn't seem to hold any resentment to the family. That was good, because family is exactly what she was now.

As he opened the door to the restaurant, he scanned the room looking for his brothers. Unfortunately, he seemed to be the first to arrive. A beautiful brunette approached him.

"Table for one?" she asked. He didn't answer. There was something very familiar about her. As he stared at her she said, "You might be more comfortable at a table." He heard her mumble, "One facing a wall."

"You work here?" he asked.

She waved the menus in the air and said, "Great guess. And if you let me seat you, I can even take your order and bring you food too."

Dylan didn't like snarky, but then again, she probably didn't enjoy being stared at either. "I'm sorry. I thought you were someone else."

Shrugging, she said, "I guess I have one of those faces. Will you be eating alone this evening?"

He wished he was. Somehow, he had a feeling having her as his waitress would be much more fun if he were. "No. I'm meeting my family, however I don't see any of them yet."

"The Lawson family?"

He nodded. "At least I know I have the right place."

She smiled and said, "You do. Follow me and I'll show you to your table." Once he was seated, she asked, "Can I get you something to drink while you wait?"

"I'm good for now."

She put her hand on her hip and said, "You're staring again."

"You look so familiar."

"I've been working here for years. My parents own the place."

"Oh, you're Sal's sister." Dylan had been here once before for lunch with his brothers. She wasn't their waitress then. "But that can't be it. You don't look like Sal at all."

"Thank God," she laughed.

"I'm Dylan," he said, not ready for their conversation to end. It was nagging at him. There was something about her eyes that drew him to her.

"Nice to meet you. I'm Sofia, the waitress. And if I don't get back to work, that might not be the case for long. Please give me a shout if you change your mind about that drink." Sofia placed the menu down on the table and hustled off to greet more customers entering.

Any hope of getting her alone again was over. The entire

crew had arrived. When they came to the table, Rosslyn said, "We missed you in the limo."

Gareth shook his head from behind her. Dylan replied, "Sorry, I didn't want to hold you guys up."

"Looks like we're the ones who are late," Charles said.

Rosslyn shot him a look and asked, "Is that a dig at me? It's not my fault. The baby is going to come when the baby wants to."

Dylan knew he'd made the right choice now by taking his own vehicle.

"No sweetheart. I said *we*, that meant all of us," Charles said softly.

Gareth walked around the table and took the seat near him. In a low voice, he said, "I'm riding back with you."

Dylan didn't respond. The last thing he wanted was for Rosslyn to overhear them. Charles held the chair for her as she wiggled her way into the seat.

Picking up the menu, she said, "I wonder if there is anything on the menu that would help me go into labor."

"If there is, you should order it to go," Seth laughed. Rosslyn shot him a look and he said, "Just saying, you're not next door to your hospital."

Rosslyn nodded. "I'm sorry guys. My due date was last week, and I guess I'm a bit…testy right now."

No one said a word. Whatever they said, wouldn't have been right anyway. Thankfully the owner arrived at their table.

"Well look at you Rosslyn. You're just glowing," Maria said.

Rosslyn smiled and said, "Oh mama, I don't feel glowy. I feel like a whale."

"Of course you do. We all do when it's that time. Ok.

Stand up and let me take a look at you." Charles helped his wife back up to her feet and Rosslyn stood there. Maria put her hands on Rosslyn's stomach and said, "Eat hardy tonight Rosslyn, because you're having this baby tomorrow."

Rosslyn beamed with joy and placed her hands on her stomach too. "Really? Tomorrow? Are you sure?"

"Of course I'm sure," Maria boasted. Charles helped Rosslyn back onto her chair. "You boys better not have plans tomorrow, because you're about to become an uncle."

Dylan looked at his brothers and they all sat tight-lipped. None of them were about to question it, not even Charles.

Rosslyn said, "Then I better have the lasagna, the pasta and meatballs, the cheesecake, and maybe the—"

"Easy sweetheart," Charles said.

"You think that's too much?" Rosslyn asked.

"No. Just want you to save room for ice cream on the way home," Charles added.

Rosslyn leaned over and kissed Charles. "I love the way you think."

Although Dylan enjoyed seeing his brother happy, this wasn't how he wanted to spend his night. "When you guys are finished, do you think you can clue us in on why you called this meeting?"

Charles reached over and placed his hand over Rosslyn's. "Since it looks like we're having a baby tomorrow, then I'm glad we're meeting tonight. I decided to take a few weeks off to be home with Rosslyn after the baby is born."

You could've heard a pin drop. Charles had been focused on the company for as long as Dylan could recall. Charles was changing, and Dylan had to admit, he was a bit concerned. "Who's taking over while you're away?" It was a valid question, and as far as Dylan thought, it was something they should've discussed a long time ago.

"Mom and Dad are coming up to New York for a few months. Mom can't wait to be a grandmother, like you guys haven't figured that out already."

"They are coming here?" Dylan looked to Gareth, knowing that was going to make their plan a bit more difficult. He'd been hoping to get Dad alone and ask questions. "And Dad is doing what exactly?"

Charles replied, "He's bored and wanted to dabble a bit in the business. It's not long term, just something to do while he's here."

Seth laughed. "And letting him hold on to the reigns of Lawson Steel was the best thing you could come up with?"

Gareth added, "I have to agree with Seth. We're taking the company in a different direction. He didn't like our ideas a few years ago, what makes you think he'll be agreeable now?"

"I don't," Charles said flatly. "That's why I need you five to make sure he doesn't fuck it up while I'm gone."

"Charles, that baby," Rosslyn warned with her hand on her stomach.

Oh, this is going to be fun. If Charles had to watch what he said before the baby was born, Dylan could only imagine what it was going to be like after.

Rosslyn looked across the table directly at Dylan, as though she could read his thoughts. "That goes for you too. I don't want our son or daughter around such language."

Dylan waited for her to threaten them with washing their mouth out with soap and water, but she didn't. From the look in her eyes, she didn't need to. The saying was true: you don't mess with a mama. They are fierce creatures who will do anything to protect their young. However, this child was half Lawson, and they were very capable of holding their own. It was a good thing too, because they'd proven to be stubborn and, at times, one hundred percent jackasses. In business it worked well. In relationships, not at all.

"I promise, I'll be on my best behavior," Dylan committed, knowing that still wasn't saying much.

"I really hope so, because I need to ask a huge favor Dylan."

Swearing wasn't enough? "I'll see if I can help."

Rosslyn smiled. "I'm hoping you can step in and watch things at Grayson Corp. for me while I'm home too?"

"Me? There isn't someone within Grayson Corp. who would be better suited?"

"I'm sure there is, but suited is one thing, trust is another. I spoke to Charles at length about this, and he informed me you might be the one most willing to take on such a challenge."

Great Charles. Now you have confidence in me. A year ago, Dylan had been out to prove to his brother that he could run the company as well, if not better, than he did. Now he wasn't so sure he wanted the job. And either way, he definitely didn't want it at their former competitor.

"Rosslyn, you taking over the company was one thing, you're a Grayson. I'm not sure putting a Lawson in charge, even temporarily, would be wise. What makes you think they'll listen to a word I say?"

"First of all, they weren't that fond of my Uncle Max. They did what he said because they feared him. That's not how I run the place. I run it with mutual respect.

Naïve. They will eat you up and spit you out. They may have feared her uncle, but they stayed out of greed. They loved the money more than anything else. It was a lesson she was going to learn, and hopefully Charles could help ease the pain when she did. There was no room for friendship in business.

Maybe she was right, and he was the correct person for the job. It'd give him a chance to feel things out at Grayson Corp. and set a few people straight who might think she didn't have some serious backing on her side. It shouldn't matter what name was on the side of the building. Rosslyn was a Lawson now, and her company now fell under their protective umbrella. *I just hope I don't sink it while she's gone.*

"You're having a baby tomorrow, remember? When do you think you'll need me there?" Dylan asked.

"Tomorrow," she grinned. "Don't worry. I have my assistant Liz ready and able to help you with whatever you need. She's been with the company for long time and knows just about everyone in the building."

"So she worked for Maxwell?" Dylan asked. She nodded. That already was a flag to him. First thing Rosslyn should've done was clean house and get rid of all the people who were loyal to Maxwell. *Just filling in, not taking over.* It was going to be hard to hold back and not do a clean sweep of the place. But that would be an impulsive move, and one he didn't have the right or authority make. That didn't mean it shouldn't be done.

"I'll be there. Tell your assistant I take my coffee black."

Rosslyn laughed. "I can tell her, and she'll say you should pick it up on your way in. Liz is no pushover." There was an odd expression that came over her face, then her eyes widened. "Charles, I think we need to call this dinner meeting short."

"What's wrong sweetheart?" he asked.

"I think my water just broke."

Charles was up and out of his seat barking orders as though Rosslyn was about to have the baby right there in the restaurant. Maria came out of the kitchen when she heard all the commotion and took control, not that she was any quieter than Charles was. Dylan stepped back and let them sort it out. This wasn't his wife and delivering a baby wasn't going to happen. Hell, he didn't even want to witness it.

"Don't worry. My mother will have them all calmed down and on their way before you know it," Sofia said softly next to him.

He'd been so distracted with all the shouting that he hadn't even heard her approach. "I'm surprised you're not over there helping."

She wrinkled her nose and said, "I'm a waitress, not a doctor. Besides, I haven't had a baby. What do I know about it?" *Probably more than me.* "Why don't you come over to the other side of the room and I'll get you that drink. You look like you could use one right now."

"I think you're right." He followed her and sat at the bar.

"What can I get you?" she asked.

"Anything on tap." Right now, he wasn't picky. If he was home, he'd have a shot of bourbon or two. But not only was he driving, he needed a clear head in case something did go wrong and he was needed. Not that he could do anything, but at least he'd be focused enough to know it.

Sofia handed him a glass of beer and then said, "She's going to be fine. Women have babies all the time."

"I'm not worried about Rosslyn; it's my brother that looks like hell. I'm not sure he's ready."

Sofia chuckled softly. "I think all expectant fathers look like that. It's the only time you have absolutely no control over anything and you can't stand it."

Dylan turned to her to correct that statement, but then realized she was right. Charles wasn't getting soft on them, he was just out of his element. Babies weren't like constructing a building. You can plan on things, but they turn out the way they want, no matter what.

"And this is why I'm staying single," Dylan said and guzzled his beer.

She raised her glass of water and said, "Me too."

When Dylan turned back, he saw Charles helping Rosslyn out the door. His four other brothers stood there, just watching. "You might want to pour four more. I think we're about to get company."

Sofia looked at the men then went back around the bar and did as Dylan suggested. Even before they had taken a seat, their tallboy beers were lined up and ready.

Seth, Jordan, and Ethan grabbed their beers and didn't say a word. Gareth, on the other hand, did. "So this is why you left us in such a hurry." If there was a pretty woman in a fifty-mile radius, Gareth didn't miss it. "And what is your name?"

"Can't you see that she's already interested in Dylan?" Jordan stated as he sipped his beer.

Gareth laughed. "It's not too late. I'm a much better dancer than Dylan is."

Sofia didn't even look in Gareth's direction as she answered. "I'm not much of a dancer anyway." Then she left them all and headed back to the kitchen.

Gareth slapped Dylan on the back and said, "Well, she put me in my place."

And I got to see it. That was going down as the highlight of his day. Gareth was a self-proclaimed ladies' man. His track record did kind of back him up on that. Dylan was glad Sofia wasn't interested in Gareth. Someone like her...he'd just break her heart.

"She's hands off for all of us," Dylan said.

Ethan asked, "All of us? Why is that?"

"She's Sal's kid sister."

"Oh…" they said in unison.

Although they didn't know much about Sal, Charles had mentioned how protective he was of his family. It wouldn't be wise for any of them to contemplate a casual fling with her. And since it didn't appear that any of them were looking for anything more, the subject was over.

Seth finished his beer and said, "I'm not sure if any of you have thought about this, but Charles left with the limo. What car did you bring Dylan?"

"The Austin-Healy. You guys aren't riding with me," Dylan stated.

Gareth laughed. "Except for me. I already claimed it earlier. We have some unfinished business to discuss."

Seth shook his head. "Why do I have a feeling you two are not discussing business?"

"Maybe we're going to be discussing Sofia?" Gareth joked.

Seth shook his head. "No. I think there's something else going on. Want to tell us about it?"

No. "Gareth and I were planning a little trip together. Which, of course, won't be happening now."

Ethan chuckled. "If I were you, I'd go anyway. No way would I want to get tangled up in that Grayson mess. The feds are still looking into some of the illegal shit Maxwell did before he died."

"Has anyone even considered how this might look? We were the ones who turned the evidence over to the feds, and now we're linked to the Grayson Corp. I'd question it if it were me," Jordan said.

"You guys make it sound like I *want* to do this. Hell, how was I going to say no to a woman who was about to deliver a baby?" Dylan said.

"Easy. N. O. It's not like she was going to freak out or anything. She's busy thinking about her breathing and shit like that now," Jordan added.

Dylan cocked a brow. "You seem to know a lot about this stuff. Why is that? Is there something we don't know about you?"

Jordan got up and said, "Yeah. I read the information that Rosslyn had sent us regarding what to expect when someone you love is expecting."

Dylan and Gareth looked at each other and burst out laughing. "I'm not even sure Charles read it."

Jordan growled. "He's the one who told me I had to read it and give him the short version of what it said."

Seth laughed. "And you did it?"

Jordan shrugged. "I was bored."

Gareth said, "I think you need to start hanging out with me. I have a few ideas to fix that boredom."

"Thanks Gareth, but I don't need your help in that department. I was actually talking about work. Things have been going so smoothly lately that it's...dull."

"Don't worry. Dad's flying in. That's all about to change." Unfortunately, that was truer than he wished. Their father wasn't coming up just to see the new baby, and Dylan knew it. What was really behind the lengthy visit? He hoped whatever it was he'd been hiding wasn't behind it all.

There's only one way to find out. Sit down with him.

Their phones all buzzed at the same time.

WE'RE AT THE HOSPITAL. TELL MARIA SHE WAS RIGHT. LOOKS LIKE THE BABY WILL BE BORN TOMORROW.

"Well, that's our cue to call it a night," Dylan said. At least it was his excuse to get out of there. He wished he'd have bumped into Sofia again, but maybe it was better that he didn't. Something in those sweet eyes of hers seemed like they could be more trouble than they were worth. *But sweet trouble all the same.*

3

Sofia had to admit, getting up before the crack of dawn to help her mother crack eggs for breakfast was going to take a bit of getting used to. It was only ten and her eyes were burning from lack of sleep. Of course, it didn't help that she had tossed and turned all night.

Dreams haunted her again. That money she'd been given, five hundred dollars, needed to get out of her apartment. It didn't belong to her. The stranger had thought he was helping someone in need. That's exactly where the money should go, to the homeless.

Her mind was made up. After her shift, Sofia was making a quick stop at her apartment for the money, then heading into the city and dropping off the money. The coins from that sweet little girl, well, that was different. Sofia had put them in her jewelry box. Although it didn't add up to even a dollar, it was priceless to her. It would always be a reminder of what a true compassionate heart was.

"You don't have to stay, you know. You covered for me by coming in early. That's why I'm here now. I owe you," Emily said.

Sofia smiled. "I really appreciate you doing this. But it's going to be a real long shift Emily."

"Oh I know. And one day I might have to ask for another favor. So please, let me pay this debt while I can. Besides, things are slow today. Your mother will freak out if she sees staff hanging around with nothing to do."

"Don't I know it. The last time, she pulled out the silverware and had me shine them all again, even though they were already spotless," Sofia said with a sigh. "If you're sure, then I'll go. There are a few things I needed to take care of anyway."

"Hopefully something fun," Emily stated.

Sofia took off her apron and hung it on the hook on the wall. "If you insist, then I'm out of here." She knew better than to just leave. Popping her head into the kitchen, she said, "Mama, Papa, Emily is here and I'm heading home."

"Okay. Go and have some fun. I'll see you in the morning," Mama shouted across the room, not even looking up from her pasta machine.

As she headed out of the restaurant, she couldn't help but wonder, why was everyone telling her to have fun? She had a life. So what, she hadn't been out for a while, but that was the price for working nights. Emily was about to learn that herself. The difference was, Emily probably would've been home with her little girl if she wasn't working. Sofia had no responsibilities except for herself. Not even a pet.

She looked at her watch. It was too early to call Charlene to do anything; she was still at work. Sal was on duty too, not that hanging out with her brother was considered fun. Sitting in her car, she pondered: which thing on her list did she hate least? Getting chores done might not be fun, but hell, it was productive at least. *Laundry. Hate it. Food shopping. I can eat at the restaurant. Housework. No one sees the place anyway.* So much for her list. Nothing appealed to her.

As she placed her purse on the passenger's seat, it tipped over. She tried to grab the wallet, but her hand got tangled in the straps and the wallet tumbled to the floor. Change went in one direction and the bills in the other. There was no longer a need to wonder what her plans were.

Leaning over, she scooped everything up and crammed it into the purse. She'd sort out the mess later. Right now she wanted to get out of this uniform and get on her way to the city. It was time to make a difference in someone's life.

While she was in the city, it might be a good idea to check out things around the theater. Sofia had been many times to see shows, but she always went directly home afterwards. Rehearsals could run late, and she wanted to make sure she found a coffee shop close by. The last thing she needed was to fall asleep behind the wheel. It'd be great if she could take a break from the restaurant altogether, but she was thankful that Emily needed to switch. The stars were all lined up in her favor, and she wasn't going to miss out on one thing this adventure was about to bring.

Once she had scoped out what she needed nearby, she decided to make one more stop before heading home. Sofia was tempted to hand the money over to the person who had been sleeping in the cardboard box in the alley. That would help, but not enough. It wouldn't help get them off the street, maybe one night, but not permanently. This had to go to a place that would take care of many, not just one.

If she were back home, she'd know exactly where to go. Here in the city was a different story. So, she did the only thing she could and pulled out her cell to search for a local soup kitchen, one that fed the poor. There wasn't anything like that close by. These were all backed by large companies and one that looked very familiar, Lawson Steel.

It was nice to learn Sal's friends weren't just rich, arrogant bastards. They were giving back to the community. Of course in her eyes, that was easy to do when you have more money than God. *Don't judge them for being rich.* To her it was no different than placing judgment on the homeless. What you wore and what you had didn't define who a person was. At least it shouldn't.

Sofia opted to go to one of the local charities that wasn't well known. They offered the homeless a place to shower and wash their clothes for free. They also handed out socks and such. Putting food in someone's belly wasn't the only way to help, and this seemed like the perfect fit for her. Besides, it was only eight blocks from where she was. That was walking distance.

When she arrived, Sofia found the place was extremely busy. People were lined up to use the facilities. Why hadn't she ever thought about doing such a thing back in her hometown? Maybe because they were in the restaurant business, so food was their first thought. *I'm going to need to mention this to Mama and Papa.* There was so much more they could be doing too.

Granted, they weren't rich like the Lawsons, but they never had to worry about where their next meal was coming from, and the restaurant was doing well. Her parents told her that wasn't always the case. When they first got married, they barely could pay their bills. Papa worked in a grocery store stocking shelves, and Mama in a laundromat washing and folding other people's clothes. It was their faith in each other that got them to open the restaurant. It didn't hurt any that they both were fantastic cooks. But it took a lot more than that. Years of blood and sweat, long hours and a lot of sacrifice went into making it what it was, the staple of that small community. They didn't need to be known all over, but in town, everyone knew and loved her parents.

I've got big shoes to fill. Impossible ones. That was one of the reasons why she needed to break away, make her own way. Sofia didn't want to always be referred to as the daughter of Maria and Filippo Marciano. Although she loved them and was proud of them, she needed her own identity. That wasn't going to happen back home.

"Miss, can I help you?"

Sofia turned around and saw a woman standing there wearing an apron that said, 'Make a new friend everyday'.

"Hi. I'm looking to make a donation," Sofia said. As she looked around, she added, "And give a lending hand today, if you could use one."

"Oh that would be wonderful. We are short two people today, their kids were home sick from school. What are you good at?"

"Taking orders," Sofia replied.

The woman laughed. "Then you'll do great, because Patty is great at giving them. She's the woman over there cutting hair."

"You provide haircuts too?"

"Not officially, but if someone asked, then we do what we can. No one is going to win a fashion contest here, but we know how to give a good trim. Well, at least Patty can. Don't you dare give Lori a pair of scissors. Not unless you want to wear a hat for a year." She extended a hand. "I'm Caroline."

"I'm Sofia. So nice to meet you. Can I give you a hand until Patty is free?"

Caroline said, "If you wait for that to happen, you'll never get to talk to her. Come on over, I'll introduce you." Sure enough, when Sofia got there, Patty didn't even stop. "Patty, this is Sofia. She wants to give us a hand today."

"And I have a donation as well," Sofia added. She pulled the money out of her pocket and handed it to Patty.

Patty didn't even count it as she slipped it into her apron pocket. "Thank you. I'm sure I can put this to use. Since you're here for the day, how about giving Caroline a hand? She's on laundry duty."

"I'd love to. Thank you so much for letting me help," Sofia said wholeheartedly. This was exactly how she wanted to fill her free time.

Sofia thought she'd be doing people's personal laundry, but in fact, there were a lot of linen and towels, a constant flow. She lost track of how many people had come and gone, some individuals and some families. All were welcomed without any question. By the end of the day she was exhausted. She thought waitressing was tough, but standing in one place for hours played havoc on her feet. Of course, she hadn't worn working shoes and only had on her flat, no-support sandals.

As she was about to leave, Patty called her over. "Sofia, I think this is yours. It was with the money you donated, which, by the way, was very generous, thank you."

She handed Sofia the business card. She'd forgotten all about it. The man had handed it to her telling her he'd help her get off the street. She handed it back to Patty. "The money actually came from this person. I'm just the middleman, or woman, in this case. Thank you again for letting me help."

Patty looked at the card and said, "It must be nice to have such...generous friends. We have been trying to get their support for a long time. Guess this is a good start." Patty slipped the card back into her apron and said, "I'll give him a call myself to thank him."

She was tempted to ask her not to, but what did it matter? The man had no idea who she was, and they surely weren't going to cross paths again. Even if they did, he wouldn't know who she was any more than she would recognize him. The entire thing was a blur, and it was best to keep it that way.

Before she left, Patty asked, "Would you mind if we took your picture and put it up on our wall of honor?"

"Wall of honor?" Sofia repeated, puzzled.

"Yes, it's where we put people who stop in but decide to stay. Our goal is to fill this wall up. Of course, as you can see, we have a long way to go."

Sofia looked in the direction Patty was pointing. There were about twenty photos, but room for a hundred times that amount. "Patty, I hope I didn't give you the wrong impression. I can only help today. I work full time and at night I have…rehearsals." She said the truth. No harm in that. The information wasn't going anywhere.

"I didn't expect you to."

"But I don't deserve to be on that wall. It was just *one* day."

Patty smiled. "If everyone gave one day to helping another, imagine what a beautiful place this world would be. Sofia, you *do* belong there, whether you believe it or not."

Sofia nodded and said, "If I can find time at all, I promise I'll come back."

Patty nodded. "Fate brought you through that door, and it will again."

Actually it was Google.

She stood still for a moment while Patty snapped her

picture with a camera Sofia had never used. It was something she might have found buried in her parents' closet. How was this old-fashioned instant camera even functioning? The photo slid out the front and the clarity wasn't great at all, but it was her.

Sofia handed the picture back to Patty and left so Patty could lock the doors. It had been a long day, and she was ready to get home. Yet she didn't regret it one bit. Not only was it productive and educational, but it was also the type of fun she enjoyed and needed. But right now, she needed some-thing else too....*sleep.*

Dylan had never seen Charles look as happy as he did right now, holding his baby girl.

"Guess you won't be calling her Charles. You'll have to go for number two," Gareth teased.

Rosslyn shot him a warning look. "I do hope you're joking."

Gareth grinned, "Of course I am."

Dylan knew he wasn't. It fell onto Charles to keep the name going. Since he was Charles Joseph Lawson the Seventh, he needed to ensure there was an Eighth. *I wonder if he told Rosslyn that.* From the expression on her face, he didn't think so. Right now definitely wasn't the time to bring it up, either.

"Don't you boys have something to do other than take up space in here? I'm waiting to rock my grandchild to sleep. That's not going to happen with all your chatter."

One by one they all walked over and kissed Rosslyn goodbye, then did the same to their mother. No one put up any argument, as they were all waiting for an excuse to bolt.

They were happy for Charles and Rosslyn, but nobody wanted to be in the room when she tried feeding the baby. It might be natural and the best for the baby, but he wasn't that close with his sister-in-law. Since little Penelope was starting to fuss, she was probably getting hungry. Funny, so was he.

As they stood in the parking lot, each let out a sigh of relief.

Ethan said, "I thought for sure she was going to ask me to hold her. There's no way I'm touching anything that tiny."

Seth nodded. "I've seen you fumble too many times when playing football, so that was a wise choice."

Jordan laughed. "I'm not worried about dropping her. It's the diapers. I'm in no rush to follow in their footsteps."

"I don't think any of you need to worry about it. Dylan is the next to fall," Gareth said.

"What the fuck are you talking about?" Dylan snapped.

Gareth said calmly, "We all saw it."

"Saw what?"

"The way you looked at her last night," Gareth continued.

"Who?"

They all said her name in unison. "Sofia."

Fuck. He didn't want anyone thinking there was something going on. Not that he was really worried about what Sal or Charles would say or think, but if Sofia thought he liked her, that might get her hurt in the long run.

"I was staying out of the way. Nothing more," Dylan clarified.

Ethan added, "I have to admit, you weren't paying attention to anything that was happening over at our end of the room. Maybe Gareth was right and you *are* interested in her."

He grumbled. "I definitely find her easier on the eyes than any of you guys. But that's it."

Gareth laughed and turned to the others. "Is it me or does our baby brother protest too much?"

Dylan clenched his fist. Gareth, like Charles, knew how to push his buttons. Then again, they had all been at the hospital most of the day waiting to see their new niece. Giving each other shit was something they had done since kids. Being the youngest, they usually avoided giving it to him. Things changed as they grew older.

"I'm glad you guys have nothing better to do than stand around thinking about women, but I have a job to do. Actually, two now. If you don't mind, I'm going to go back to work."

"You don't want to join us for dinner? We're going to The Choice to celebrate," Seth said.

"Thanks, but this *baby brother* has too much to do. I'll see you in the office in the morning."

"I thought you were going to Grayson Corp," Jordan said.

"I will. But Lawson Steel comes first." *Always will.*

He left them standing there as he got into his 1966 Austin Healy 3000. He had no idea how he was going to pull this off. Dylan had no issue with working hard, he'd done it for all his adult life. He might have been born privileged, but they weren't given anything without it being earned. They were all grateful for that lesson in life. It made them strong competitors now. One thing he wasn't in the race for was getting tied down having a family. He had no problem coming in last on that list.

He just pulled out onto the main road when his phone rang. Since it was an unknown number, the Bluetooth connection didn't state the callers ID. He was tempted to ignore it, but since he'd just left the hospital, he answered anyway. Things had looked okay when he left, but life was fragile and things could change quickly.

"Lawson here."

"Hello Mr. Lawson. My name is Patty. I'm calling from 'A Fresh Day'. I'm not sure if you're familiar with us.

He wasn't in the mood for a sales call. Actually he never took them. That's what he had office staff for. They weeded through the bullshit and if there was something of importance, they gave him the details. "If you have any inquiries, you should call my office, not my personal line." Dylan said firmly. He wasn't even sure how the hell she got it.

"I'm so sorry. It was the number circled on the card."

That changed things. He only gave out that card when he *wanted* someone to have it. Even though he didn't recall giving it to that agency, he needed more information from her. "You said your name was Patty?"

"Yes sir. I was only calling to thank you for your donation. It was kind and very...unexpected. Since this is your personal line, I assume it was not through Lawson Steel."

Not even sure it was from me. "And you obtained this donation..."

"From Sofia. I didn't get her last name. A beautiful brunette maybe mid to late twenties."

There was only one person with that name who fit that description. He knew for a fact he didn't give her his cell, not that he didn't want too. "Patty, I would like to confirm the amount if you don't mind."

"Of course. It was five-hundred dollars. But I can assure you, someone as sweet as that young lady wouldn't have taken a penny. She actually stayed and worked all afternoon until closing. Wonderful girl. Her picture is hanging proudly on our wall of honor."

That was the exact amount he'd given the homeless woman with his card. There was only one way to find out who that woman was. Dylan needed to see the photo for himself. "Patty, I'd like to double that amount. Would you mind if I came by in the morning and delivered it personally?"

The excitement in her voice rang crystal clear before she could compose herself again. He got it. She wasn't thrilled about another five-hundred bucks; it was the potential of nailing him as a long term sponsor. Dylan wasn't crossing it off his list, but the sponsorship was done through the company and they decided as a family which to accept.

"Mr. Lawson, that would wonderful. Please come by any time."

"My schedule is tight. I'll see you at eight." Dylan wanted to be in and out of there. If he left it open, Patty might try to occupy more time than he wanted to give. His intentions were not what Patty believed. There was only one thing he wanted from that visit and that was to find out who the hell this Sofia woman was and how she got his number. *It couldn't be the homeless woman.* Why would she have given the money away when she obviously needed it herself?

Dylan wasn't doing anything at the moment and decided to turn his car around and take a ride by the theater where he'd seen her. If she was still out there, maybe he could ask her directly. He should've helped her then. Just handing her money and his number wasn't enough. And he also wasn't thinking. She was homeless and he gave her a card saying call me. With what? If she didn't have food, why the hell didn't he realize she probably didn't have a cell phone.

When Dylan arrived, he spent almost an hour walking the street, even checking a few back allies and she was nowhere to be found. He was pissed at himself. Dylan had put it on her to reach out when he was the one with the power and ability to actually do something positive in her life. Hindsight, he'd have done it differently. He would've stayed, followed her, done something more. What exactly that was, wasn't clear yet, but he had connections, the right people who would've known what to do. Now, finding her again in New York City was near to impossible. And all he had to go on was the beautiful tearful eyes to remind him of his mistake.

It was too early to call it a night and he hadn't even stopped to eat. Since his apartment contained only the basic needs, like coffee and beer, he knew he needed to stop. The guys would probably still be at The Choice, but he wasn't in the mood for that either. There was a place which did appeal to him. The home cooked feeling. It was out of his way, but worth the drive. With any luck, it would be slow there tonight and Sofia and he could finish that drink they started yesterday.

This had nothing to do with him being interested in her either. There was nothing wrong with sitting and having a nice conversation over dinner with someone who was attractive. It didn't mean he had to take her home and sleep with her. It also didn't mean the thought hadn't crossed his mind. But in his imagination was the only place he'd be having sex with her.

When he pulled up to the restaurant he noticed Sal's car parked in the lot. For a second he questioned if going inside was a good idea. Then again, why shouldn't he? He'd already made up his mind that nothing was going to happen between him and Sofia. Besides, he was hungry and Maria knew how to cook.

As he entered, Sal called him to over. "What brings you here?"

"Your mothers cooking."

Sal nodded. "Watch out. I swear she puts something

inside that gets you addicted. People try to stay away, but they can't."

"We were here last night, but none of us got to eat." Dylan said.

"I heard. Congratulations on being an uncle." He shook his head. "I still can't believe Charlie is a father."

Dylan wasn't used to hearing his brother called Charlie. It seemed so odd, but in this place, that's how they knew him. And from what he'd learned, Sal knew a side of *Charlie* that the family didn't. Maybe that's what Rosslyn saw in him too. There had to be something, because they were so different yet for some reason, they fit. Kind of like his parents did.

Dylan pulled out his cell phone and showed Sal the picture. "I'm just glad she didn't have it here."

Sal laughed. "Mama would've loved it. The customers, not so much."

"I don't think I'd be eating here again if that table had just delivered a baby either."

Maria came over and said, "What are you doing here? Why aren't you helping your brother?"

Dylan had a few wise crack remarks, but Maria was serious. If he even joked, he wasn't getting anything to eat, paying customer or not. "We've been there most of the day. The parents wanted time alone." That had to be true. They had looked happy, but exhausted.

"I shall cook something special for them and you can bring it to them."

"Maria I"

"Mama. Everyone calls me Mama," she corrected.

"Mama, they won't be home for a few days."

"Yes. True. Okay, you must come back Friday and I'll have meals for a week for them."

She turned and walked away before he could tell her there

was no need. Dylan turned to Sal and said, "They don't need it."

"Do you want to tell her no?" Sal asked. Dylan shook his head. "Good, because I sure in hell wasn't going to do it for you. She's one of those Italian women who like to, no have to, feed you. And if you're smart, you eat it, no questions."

"You're sister kind of gave me that speech last night."

"Sofia?"

"You only have one right?" Dylan asked.

"Yes. I didn't realize you two were…talking," Sal said with a questioning look on his face.

Dylan had to remember that Sal was a cop and it was his job to read people. "She was our waitress last night. When all the commotion broke out, she had the same deer in the head-light look that I did."

Sal said, "I'm glad I missed it. I can't believe my mother didn't make Sofia stay there and help."

"We all wanted to help, but from a distance. Besides, your mother had everything under control."

"She always does. I'd be the best cop in town if I had my mother's sense of things. I heard she even knew when the baby was going to be born. Scary, isn't it?"

"Bet you never got away with anything when you were growing up," Dylan teased.

"Ha. I can't now either. That's why I stop in only once a week. Sofia is an angel for putting up with it all these years. I couldn't do it. Hell, I'm not even sure she wants to." Sal looked around and said, "Speaking of Sofia, I wonder where she is?"

There was a different waitress there. "Maybe it's her night off."

"She doesn't have one." Sal called the girl over. "Emily, where's my sister?"

"Oh, we switched shifts. She's working the morning shift and I have the nights. Can I get you guys anything?"

They put in their orders and Emily left. Dylan wasn't sure he was glad he'd missed Sofia or not. She definitely added something extra to the place and tonight, even though the food was great, it was lacking Sofia's charm.

4

The moment he walked into A Fresh Day he knew there was something different about this place. Of course, it wasn't open to serve the public yet, but Patty had obviously been there for hours getting the place ready for his arrival.

Dylan hated that she'd gone to so much trouble when his reasoning behind this visit had nothing to do with the facility. Normally he could blatantly brush someone off and get to the point. Patty's enthusiasm and effort made him delay asking for what he wanted.

"And this is our laundry room. We encourage people to come as often as they wish. We don't care if they have only a few items or several loads. We provide all detergent for them as well. If someone comes here with only the clothes on their back, we always make sure they leave with at least one clean set. Not always the right size, but we do the best we can. We run strictly on donations and volunteers."

"And you get paid how?" Dylan asked. She was the one who'd opened the door to that line of questioning.

"I don't. No one does. This used to be my parents' place

years ago. They owned the building and gave it to me when they retired."

He knew the location. "This is prime location for real estate. Why haven't you sold?"

Patty met him square in the eyes. "Because this is also *prime* location to help those who need it. What would another apartment complex or store that they couldn't afford to go into be to them? For me, for my family, and for all those who come and help, this place has *nothing* to do with money."

She was definitely passionate about what she was doing here. Dylan hated to admit it, but this might be something he and his brothers looked into for sponsoring. *Or maybe Grayson Corp.* They needed to change their status in the community. Rosslyn had done some things, but mostly with the staffing. How much could one pregnant woman do who had never run a company before? Charles was helping, but he also was overly distracted with adjusting to being a husband and now a father.

"I would like more information regarding this place. This isn't the best time for me, but why don't you come by the office next week? This will give you time to prepare as well."

Her eyes widened. "You're serious? You're thinking about helping us?"

"I said I'd look at your place more closely. If it is what you say, then there is a possibility you'll have a sponsor. This, however, must stay between you and me for now. I don't want anyone getting wind of it, or the meeting won't take place. Understood?" She nodded. "Good. Here is the money I had mentioned on the phone." Dylan handed her five one hundred-dollar bills. "If you don't mind, I'd like to take a look at the wall of honor you spoke about."

"Certainly. It's growing slowly, but that is okay." She led

him to a back room holding all the photos. "Not very fancy, but we don't need it to be."

Dylan scanned the pictures, bypassing the men. One woman's face leapt off the wall, and he knew right then it was ~~her.~~ *she Sofia Marciano.* What it didn't explain was how the hell she'd gotten the money and the business card. He hadn't given it to her and definitely hadn't dropped one either. No one at the restaurant had it either. *Except for my family.* Gareth was the type of guy who'd tell him not to do something, and then he'd intervene and do it for him. That had to be the explanation behind this.

"Thank you for showing me your place Patty. I'll call you when I have time to meet."

She beamed and said, "Thank you for another donation. It's going into this week's sock fund."

Socks. Simple and something he and most took for granted. A Fresh Day was doing their part to make a difference. He knew this was the perfect fit for Rosslyn. And it would give her something fun and positive to think about while home with Penelope.

He nodded and left the building. It was time for him to make a quick stop at Lawson Steel for a meeting. He needed to get Gareth alone so they could talk about their father. No matter how much was being put on his plate, Dylan wasn't going to forget this. There was something left unsaid, and it was time to find out what that was. If Gareth didn't want in on it, Dylan would face their father alone. *It wouldn't be the first time.*

As the youngest, he and his father sure as hell didn't see eye-to-eye. His mother had stepped in many times as they disputed Dylan's choice of lifestyle. Dear old Dad dressed the same way every day, acted the same too. He never raised his voice or seemed to step out of line. If you asked Dylan, he was boring as hell. The only thing he ever did was work, then come home for dinner and eat with the family, then work some more.

Dylan missed a lot of dinners, and his curfew was broken more times than it was kept. Quiet wasn't something Dylan had ever been accused of. Wherever he went, he left an impression. Not always a good one, but he believed those days were behind him. For the most part, at least.

When he arrived at Lawson Steel and walked into the boardroom, his jaw clenched. This wasn't what he wanted to see. Their father was sitting in the CEO's seat. He'd given up that spot years ago. Although Dylan had challenged whether or not Charles should fill it, that doubt no longer lingered. Lawson Steel finally was heading in the direction they'd all agreed upon. All except one. *Dad, you should be with Mom. Not here.*

It was a horrible thought, and he didn't want to seem ungrateful, but they didn't need their father's help. Actually, during his reign, the company had slipped backwards. Their grandfather ran a much tighter ship and was an aggressive businessman. Dad was intelligent, but forceful? Not even close. *And I want to know why.*

Sitting down even now and listening to his father talk, it wasn't as though he were in charge. If any of them spoke up and pushed back, Dylan didn't think there would be much of a fight. If this was going to be long term, he would've spoken up. But right now no one wanted to rock the boat and bring any unneeded stress onto Charles. So they all shut their mouths and ignored what they could.

"Any questions before I go and visit my grandson?"

"Granddaughter, Dad," Ethan corrected.

Their father huffed. "Wishful thinking I guess."

Don't let Charles hear you say that. "I don't know, she's

kind of cute. Besides, you had six boys, I'd think you were ready for a girl."

"That's not how this works," he replied.

Seth laughed. "Dad, I think you need to read up on this, because that's exactly how it works."

Shooting Seth a warning glance, he said calmly, "You know what I mean. The Lawson name is everything."

Dylan spoke up. "Dad, it's a name. That's all."

"You should be proud of what the past generations have done. If it wasn't for their sacrifices, you might not be where you are today."

They all knew how hard everyone had worked to keep the company going since 1808. That is no small feat. "We know Dad. You told us the stories many times."

"Ha. Only some of them." In a softer voice he added, "Only what I could."

The brothers all looked at each other, puzzled by that statement. This only made Dylan even more curious than before. Maxwell Grayson was able to cover his dirty little secrets for a long time. What had the Lawson family been hiding?

When he left the boardroom, Gareth said, "Glad that's over."

"Over? This is just the beginning. We have weeks of this crap," Jordan said. "I don't know about you, but I'm not starting each morning like this. If I do, I won't be motivated to go out and do any *real* work."

Seth added, "I agree. Who's going to tell Dad we don't need him?"

They all looked at Gareth, who was the second oldest. He shook his head. "You're not pawning this off onto me. We can tell him at tomorrow's meeting. *Together.*"

"I'll do it," Dylan offered. They looked at him like they

were hearing things. "I need to talk to him anyway." He got up from his seat and said, "Don't worry, I'll have some tact."

Gareth laughed. "That's not your strong point, Dylan."

Jordan interjected. "Hey, he wants to do it, let him. Someone has to, or we'll all be out of a job. I don't know about you, but I worked too fucking hard on that contract to let Dad blow it now."

Ethan said, "Agreed. Did you want me to go with you Dylan?"

He really wanted Gareth's backing, but since that didn't seem to be happening, Dylan opted to do it alone. "I got this. Tomorrow morning, things will be as usual."

Seth got up to head for the door with Dylan saying, "I sure as hell hope so, or I'm not going to be here. I love Dad and everything, but working for him, it's not going to happen. I have no idea how Charles did it all those years."

"Just think, if it hadn't been Charles, it might have been one of us," Gareth said solemnly. "I have a feeling there is a lot our brother did for us that we don't know about."

Dylan agreed. Somehow the Lawsons were filled with secrets, and his gut said none of them were good.

"I've got to go. Liz from Grayson is already wondering where I am," Dylan said, grateful for the excuse to get out of there.

Gareth laughed. "You just got the women beating down your door, don't you?"

Dylan could still hear Gareth's laugh as he walked down the hall. Oh yeah, the women all wanted something from him. Work. It wasn't that he wanted anything more with them, Rosslyn and Liz were both spoken for and neither his type. But working so much was putting a crimp in his lifestyle. All work and no play was making Dylan one frustrated man. He needed to unwind, and he knew just where he wanted to do that. Too bad she switched shifts and wouldn't be at the restaurant tonight. *At least I can get a good meal, if nothing else.*

On his way to Grayson Corp., Dylan called his father. "What about lunch today Dad? There are a few things I need to talk to you about."

"Should I bring your mother? You know she's always the best with advice."

That was true. "No Dad. This is work related."

Mom never got involved in business stuff. Dylan wasn't sure if it was because Dad never allowed her to, or if she really wasn't interested. Either way, she was retired now, and it was too late to start.

"Tell me where and I'll meet you."

"The Choice at two." Dylan didn't want to pull him away from Penelope immediately, but he also knew Charles and Rosslyn would need the break.

"Two o'clock. I'll see you then."

Everything was so formal, as though it were any regular business meeting and they weren't related. The warmth in the house had all been their mother. Their comical sense of humor, also from their mother. She had a way of always looking on the bright side of things. He hoped she would understand what he had to tell Dad, because it wasn't going to go over well.

The rest of the morning was uneventful compared to how it had started. Although he had asked Patty to prepare a presentation for him, he didn't leave anything to chance. He spent hours online researching and pulling documents to back up what she had told him.

Everything seemed legit. Now the only thing he needed to know was why Sofia chose that place to leave his card. He could speculate, but would rather just ask her. When he was finished speaking with his father, he was going to make one more stop, the restaurant. Dylan wasn't sure if Maria or Filippo would give him her number, but it was worth asking.

His reminder on his phone chimed letting him know it was time to meet with his father. Dylan had been ready to tackle everything today, but that was probably more than his father could handle. So once again, Dylan's list of questions was going to need to wait. Another day or two wasn't going to change anything.

The Choice was only a two-block walk from Grayson Corp., and it didn't take him long to meet up with his father. Of course, Dylan had run a few minutes late and his father hated being kept waiting.

"You're late."

"Have you ever known me to be on time?" Dylan asked.

He laid down the menu and said in a serious tone, "You're running a multi-billion-dollar company. I'd have thought that would mean something to you."

"Dad, this is lunch. You make it sound like I'm blowing off the deal of the century."

"Dylan, you need to take things more seriously."

"And Dad, you need to learn how to loosen up." This was a good intro to what he needed to say. "Things are different at Lawson Steel now."

"So I see."

"I'm glad you do. We…function differently than before. It might not be what you're used to or what you want, but it works for us."

He stared at Dylan and asked, "What are you trying to say?"

Dylan wasn't really firing his father. It was more like… *Shit. I'm firing him.* "Dad, you should enjoy this time with Penelope and leave Lawson Steel to us."

"That is your mother's job."

"And running the company is *ours*."

"I ran that company for more years than you have been alive," he said firmly.

"Dad, you handed over the reins for a reason. Now it's time to let go. We know what we're doing and—"

"You don't need me."

When said like that, Dylan felt like an ass. He needed to watch his next statement, or his dad would be right back in the office tomorrow, raring to go. "Dad, if you didn't think we could do this, you never would've stepped down." That was all he had. Putting the decision back on his father. Either he was wrong then, or wrong now.

"I can see why they sent you."

"What do you mean?" Dylan asked.

"You're not afraid to do what needs to be done. That doesn't mean I agree with you, but I'll respect your decision. I will not be in the office tomorrow or any other day. Not unless one of you calls and asks for my assistance."

"Thanks Dad."

"Are we still eating, or was this just a ruse to get me to meet you?"

Dylan shook his head. "I'd have suggested coffee if that were the case."

He picked up his menu and said, "Good, because I've missed this place."

It was the closest he was going to get to his father saying he wanted to spend time with them. *Me too Dad.*

Sofia was exhausted and had almost been asleep when Emily called asking her to come to the restaurant. What change did she need now? There was no way another shift change could be happening so soon, could it?

When she walked in, she headed towards Emily. Emily pointed to a table by the stone fireplace. Was that Dylan there sitting alone? Looking back at Emily she smiled and nodded then disappeared into the kitchen.

Sofia walked over and said, "Is this seat taken?"

Dylan looked up and waved his hand for her to take a seat. "I thought you didn't work evenings any longer."

Sofia smiled. "I don't. Tonight I'm a patron, just like you. Have you eaten yet?"

Dylan replied, "I'm sure I can handle another helping."

She laughed. "No one leaves without at least two if my mother can help it." She got up and he grabbed hold of her hand.

"Leaving me already?" Dylan asked.

"I was going to get us something to eat."

Dylan waved his free hand and Emily came rushing over. "Hi. I think we're ready to order."

Sofia felt so funny sitting back down and giving her order to another waitress. If her mother saw this she'd flip out. Emily had her pad out and pen in hand, as though this were an everyday occurrence. She still didn't know why Emily had even called her.

When she left to hand in their order, Sofia got up and said, "The bar is closed, but since I know the owner, I think they won't mind if I grab us each a beer."

"Sounds good."

Sofia motioned for Emily to come nearby so they could speak. "Emily what is going on here?"

"Duh. Open your eyes."

"They are, but only because you called me. I thought there was something wrong."

"Did I say there was?" Emily asked.

"No, but you never call me in unless there is an issue." Usually to cover a shift.

"Well when someone that looks like he does comes in and asks me for your number, I figured that was a good enough reason to drag you back here."

"He asked you for my number?" She had no idea why.

"No. I heard him ask your mother. I thought for sure she was going to chew him out. Instead she ignored it and brought him food."

That was even more puzzling. "Did you hear anything else, like why he wanted my number?"

Emily chuckled. "Since he's sitting right there all alone and waiting for you, why don't you ask him yourself?"

"I think you have been working for my mother too long."

"Oh no. I was this way long before I met her. Just ask my husband." Emily laughed. Before she walked away she added, "Why don't you get back to that cutie over there before he thinks you don't like him."

Sofia would expect this type of behavior from Charlene, not a coworker. Of course, they were all like family at Mama's Place, but she'd prefer everyone butting out of business. They weren't thinking correctly. That guy wasn't just a patron, he was Dylan Lawson. People like him aren't interested in people like her. That did leave the question as to why he wanted her number. With beers in hand she returned to the table. Not because he was a cutie, and he most definitely was, but because she had some questions for him.

Handing him his beer, she sat back down. "I was just talking to Emily and she informed me you wanted my number. I guess this wasn't just some chance meeting."

Dylan shook his head. "Not quite. I wanted to speak to you."

"Here I am."

"I received a call from A Fresh Day yesterday to thank me for a donation."

She smiled just hearing the name. "It's a wonderful place. I've been there."

"So I've heard. Patty couldn't stop raving about you."

"Me?" She was confused. Sofia had only given her first name, nothing more. How was it that Dylan knew she'd been there? Then panic hit her. She didn't want anyone to know. How was she going to explain being in the city when she said she was going home? In a softer voice she said, "I hate to ask, but can we change the subject?"

Dylan eyed her but nodded. "Patty called my personal cell phone."

"Oh." She wasn't sure if he'd gotten the point about not talking about this.

"Yes. She told me she got it from you. I'm sure you can imagine how surprised I was. I wasn't even aware you had my number."

Neither was I. "I'm sure she was mistaken."

"No. Patty was positive about it. Do you know what's even more puzzling?" She didn't want to know. But by the look on Dylan's face, he was about to tell her. "She said you handed it to her with a donation from me."

Her mind raced in a million directions. The money she'd handed Patty was the money she'd gotten from a stranger. Dylan was that person? He'd stopped and helped a beggar on the street? *God, you're not just gorgeous, but you're kind and generous too.* He sure seemed to be the whole package. And what was she? Oh, a fake. How could she tell him without pissing him off? She had taken his money under false pretenses. Granted, she didn't keep it for herself and actually put it to use in a way she hoped he approved of, but that didn't make any difference.

"Dylan, I really prefer not to talk about this. At least not here." Emily was still watching them from a distance.

"Would you like to take a walk?" Dylan asked.

Well that answered that. He wasn't dropping it for anything.

"This is why you wanted my number?" she asked.

"It is."

So much for being flattered that he might be interested in her. Sofia closed her eyes for a moment, knowing this charade was over. Once Dylan knew, then so would others and before long, her parents would learn the truth. She opened her eyes and said, "Let me tell my mother we're taking our food to go."

"If you'd prefer to eat first that is fine."

Her stomach was tossing and turning already. Eating was the last thing she wanted. "I don't think that's a good idea."

"How about we just step outside for a few minutes?"

She looked around and because it was late, not many people were there. She called out to Emily and said, "We're going for a short walk. We'll be right back."

Emily grinned and said, "Take your time."

Dylan let her lead the way as they went outside. She knew there were some benches across the street and that was probably going to have to do. She wasn't about to ask to go sit in his car. That would just cause people to speculate that they were making out. That wasn't about to happen.

Once they were seated, she started to explain. "That was me in the city. I was the woman begging on the street."

"You? Why?" Dylan looked around, knowing it made no sense.

"I want to be an actress and I was at the theater for a part in a play. They weren't sure about me, so they wanted me to prove I had what it took. If I could get five people to give me money as a homeless person, the part was mine."

She could feel him glare at her. "Well you did a great job at hustling people out of money."

"No, that's not what I was trying to do."

"But you took money under false pretenses. What else would you call it?" Dylan asked.

Her heart felt heavy; she knew he was right. "I'm…sorry. I wanted the part so badly that I wasn't thinking of how the people who gave me money might feel."

Dylan stared at her for what seemed to be an eternity. "Why didn't you call me and return it?"

"I never even looked at the card. Actually, I forgot all about it. I knew the money wasn't mine to keep. And I wanted whoever, now that being you, to have actually given it to the needy. So, I went back into the city and found a place where I could do that." She was being so truthful with him and hoped he could find it in him to forgive her. No one liked being lied to or manipulated. "I never did anything like that before, and I swear, I won't again." No part was worth this feeling she had inside.

"So why couldn't we discuss this inside?" Dylan asked.

Oh the real hard part hits now. "That's another story. See, my parents would never understand me going into the city to do this. They want me to stay here and run the restaurant when they retire. That's not what I want."

"Just explain to them. I'm sure they'll understand."

Dylan made it sound so easy. "No. They won't. I've tried for years. And then they would tell Sal, and he'd tell them how dangerous it was for me to be alone in the city so late at night. And before you know it, I'm stuck here for the rest of my life."

"You're not a child. You don't need permission to do what you want."

Sofia chuckled. "Have you met my family? Because you sound like you haven't. I can't let them know. Not now at least. They somehow would block this chance for me, like by putting me back on the night shift, or by Sal using his connections to get me kicked out of the play."

"I'd like to think you're being dramatic, but I've spoken to your mother a few times. She can be…"

"Tough as nails. She'll give a person the shirt off her back, but she is so stubborn. It's like she can block out anything she doesn't want to hear." *Like me telling her I don't want to do this anymore.*

"So what are you going to do?" Dylan asked.

"I guess that depends on you really. Will you help me keep my secret?" She wouldn't allow herself to be hopeful. There was no reason why he should say yes. Sofia wasn't the type who would bat her eyelashes and flirt to get what she wanted either.

"So you want my help continuing on with this charade?" Dylan asked. She nodded. "Hell, why not. What do I need to know or do?"

She was so thrilled she threw her arms around his neck and gave him a quick hug. "God you're a life saver. Thank you so much. I haven't really thought it out. I guess you don't say anything, that's all."

"And how are you going to explain being in the city so much?" he asked.

"I'm hoping they don't find out. Guess that's ridiculous. Maybe I can say I picked up another job."

"No. They will just have you work more hours here. Why don't you say we're dating, and you were with me?"

Dylan said it so quickly that she barely could process it. "I'm not sure I understand."

"If they think you're alone, they'll worry. If you're with me, they won't."

Sofia laughed. "No. But there are worse things than them being worried about me." *They might actually hope we are serious about each other.* "I don't know about your parents, but mine would start planning for grandkids."

Dylan choked. "Mine too." They sat quietly for a minute and then he said, "I only see the two options: you either tell them the truth, or we roll the dice and let them think we're dating."

She peered at him. "Why would you do this for me?" Sofia knew he wanted something, but what was it?

"Consider it a thank you for delivering my donation to A Fresh Day."

"That's it?" she asked.

He leaned over, tipped her chin up closer to him, and said, "And maybe this." Dylan placed the sweetest, gentlest kiss on her lips that left her head spinning. Sofia didn't want it to end, but he pulled away and said, "We better get back inside before our dinner is cold."

He got up and offered her a hand to get up as well. She took it but made sure to let go right away. Sofia felt as though all eyes were on her, and she wasn't ready to initiate Dylan's plan. This was stupid. All she was doing was adding another level of complexity to something that should be simple. *Grow some and just tell them the truth.* Even as she lectured herself, she knew she had to, just not today.

As they returned to their table, her mother came out. "Well I was wondering when you two were going to return. When Emily told me you went for a walk, I thought there was something wrong."

"Sorry Mama. We just wanted to talk."

"And you can't do that here?" she asked.

No. "Mama, we just wanted to be alone for a minute. That's all."

Maria looked at Dylan closely then beamed a smile. "I understand. I was young too once upon a time. But next time, wait till after dinner."

Dylan nodded, "We will."

We. She didn't want to think about a next time. But she had to admit, Dylan could smile and charm her mother very easily. That might be exactly what she needed to pull this off. It was only for a few months. After the play, everything could go back to normal. *I just don't want normal any more.*

When they were alone, Dylan leaned over and said, "If you want to keep that part, you better work on your acting skills. Dating, remember?"

She was about to give him a piece of her mind when she noticed the curl of his lips. But he was right. Sofia needed to work on it. He was going to pay for that little comment. And since this *dating* idea was his, she knew exactly who to call on to run through her lines.

Smiling at him, she leaned over closer to him and said, "I'm saving it for the stage."

He said softly, "Practice makes perfect."

Sofia whispered, "Be careful. You don't even know what part I have yet."

His eyes widened. "Damn. I was hoping it was a lover."

Giggling, she replied, "Not even close. You might want to date someone more...suitable."

He covered her hand and said, "I date who I want."

There was no hint he was joking. But this wasn't really a date. Was it? *No. He's just being nice and helping me out.* She was going to tell herself that until she believed it.

67

5

Sofia thought for sure her mother would've been asking a bunch of questions, but surprisingly, none. If anything, she seemed to be avoiding the topic altogether. Sofia wasn't sure if that was a good sign or not. Maybe her mother hadn't bought Dylan's little act and was waiting for Sofia to fess up. That wasn't about to happen any time soon.

But if she thought her day at Mama's Place was odd, her BFF's reaction really threw her.

"I can't believe this. You do know who he is, right?" Charlene said.

"Of course I do. None of it matters because it's *not* true. We are not dating," Sofia stressed for the third time.

"You can say what you want, but one thing leads to another and before you know it, he'll be rocking your world and you won't even remember your name."

"Charlene! Will you knock it off? He's helping me. That's it." Sofia didn't need any more thoughts about Dylan than she'd already had. She wasn't blind and her senses worked just fine. That kiss had her pulsing in places that wouldn't have minded a kiss or twenty either. But thoughts like that were going to make this awkward between them.

Charlene shook her head. "Oh don't you even try to pretend that you haven't thought about what it'd be like. You're not that good of an actress."

Sofia was getting tired of people saying that. Were they subtle hints that she sucked, and no one wanted to come right out and tell her? She hoped not, but it was beginning to look that way. Even the director didn't hire her immediately and made her do some foolish test. What if all this was for nothing? Maybe the restaurant was where she was meant to be. *And I should be grateful I have that.*

"Come on Sofia, you know I'm only teasing you. If you sucked, I'd be the first to tell you. That's what friends are for."

"Thanks Charlene." But Sofia wasn't so sure. Charlene wouldn't want to hurt her feelings, just like she wouldn't want to hurt hers. She remembered when they were in high school and Sofia had bought this pair of pink jeans that she loved. Charlene never told her how horrendous they looked. It was actually her brother Sal who spoke up. Charlene said they hadn't looked *that* bad. That translated to ugly as far as Sofia was concerned.

"Did you remember to bring me some cheesecake from the restaurant?"

"Charlene, you are capable of going and getting your own, you know."

"Of course I can, but why would I when I have delivery? Besides, you didn't come here just to tell me you're *not* interested in Mr. Sexy."

"Please don't call him that. His name is Mr. Lawson," Sofia said firmly. Charlene wasn't one who worried about being overheard, and she didn't want to risk Dylan ever hearing him called that. *But the name does fit.*

"Fine. Am I allowed to call him Dylan?" Charlene asked sarcastically. Sofia nodded. "Good. So tell me, when are you seeing him again?"

"I don't know. We never really discussed that part. He's got a lot going on. His brother just had a baby and he's—"

"Blah, blah blah… Sofia, do you need an intervention?"

"I'm serious. Some people have things to do besides butting into *other* people's lives," Sofia said with her hands on her hips. "I, for one, have a play to rehearse for."

"Oh, exciting. Do you need me to read through the lines with you? Tell me, did you get one with a hot love scene?"

"No, and I don't have the lead either. This is a small role, but at least I got one." Sofia never thought she'd even get that, the first time around.

"That's a positive attitude. Why don't you use that same way of thinking regarding Dylan?" Charlene suggested.

"I hope you know this is the last time I'm bringing you anything. All you've done since I got here is—"

"Encourage you to be the best you. I know you better than anyone. Actually Sofia, sometimes I think I know you better than you do yourself. You have big dreams and you want it all, but you're the one who is holding you back, not your parents. For some reason, you have doubts about your ability. That is also what makes you think you couldn't ever be with someone like Dylan." Charlene said firmly, "Trust me, he'd be lucky to have someone like you."

Sofia smirked. "I'm so not sure about that. I still feel horrible about the money."

"You were only doing as you were told to do. If anyone should feel bad, it's the director. What kind of bullshit was that? You're an amazing actress. If he wasn't smart enough to see it the first time, it was his loss. And that goes for your Mr. Sexy too. Got it?"

"Got it." Sofia was lucky to have such a cheerleader. It was undeserved, but still appreciated. "So are you going to help me run through these lines or not?"

"Sure, but I'm not promising anything."

"Please. I've seen you when you're flirting with a guy. You're a natural actress," Sofia teased.

Charlene reached behind her and threw one of the decorative pillows at her. "Hey, at least I'm out there trying. Not all of us are lucky enough to snag a billionaire." Sofia raised her finger, giving her yet another warning. "Fine. I'll stop. But it's way too easy. Besides, you should see your face each time I say it. I'm not sure you're not holding something back." Charlene leaned closer and looked her directly in the eyes. "Did he…kiss you?" Sofia tried with all her might not to look away, but she couldn't help it. "I knew it. To hell with practicing lines. Get to the juicy shit already. I'm dying over here."

"It was nothing. Just a brief kiss last night when we went to talk. That's it." Of course, the sparks from even such a short encounter still had her wanting more. That's what she couldn't afford to do. Wanting more is what had gotten her into this predicament in the first place. *Why can't I just be happy with what I have?* Right now, it was the kiss she was thinking about, not the restaurant. Charlene might be teasing her, but really, she was only saying what Sofia didn't have the guts to. With a sigh, she added, "But damn he can kiss."

Charlene winked. "I'm sure he's good at lots of things."

If I find out, I'm not telling. Her cell phone rang, thankfully. "Hi Mama, is everything all right?"

"No. Did you see the news?"

"What's wrong?" Sofia said, now filled with panic.

"Your brother Salvatore is in the city and there has been a shooting. He's not picking up his phone."

This wasn't the first time her mother had freaked out. It must be difficult having your son as a policeman in such tough times. "Mama, Sal doesn't work in the city." Hopefully that eased her mind.

"He went to see the new baby. Oh my boy. What if—"

"Mama, don't think like that. He probably shut off his phone so he didn't wake the baby. I'll call Dylan now and check."

"Oh Sofia, I couldn't bear it," her mama said, voice shaking.

"I know, Mama. And trust me, Sal is okay. I'll call you right back."

She immediately called Dylan. Her mother was right, it was good to check on people you cared about. "Hi Dylan, I'm calling to check and make sure everything is okay with you. You and your family." She didn't want it to sound as if she wasn't concerned about all the Lawsons equally.

"We're fine. Why?"

"My mother said there was a shooting and she is worried because she can't reach Sal. He's supposed to be with Charlie. Can you please do me a favor and ask your brother if Sal is there safe and sound?"

"Of course. Hold on a minute."

It seemed like forever while she waited, knowing her mother would be counting the seconds. When he got back on the line, she was relieved.

"Sofia, I spoke to both Charles and Sal. Sal will call your mother now. Everyone is okay. I guess he was holding Penelope."

"Thank you, Dylan. I owe you. I hope this doesn't become a habit."

"Calling me?" Dylan asked.

"No. Me owing you."

Dylan laughed. "If you want, we can chip away at that debt and you can have dinner with me."

"Dinner? Tonight?" Sofia asked.

Charlene was nodding her head and shouted, "She'll be ready."

"Charlene, stop!" Sofia said covering the phone. But it was too late.

"So, six sound good to you?" Dylan asked.

Shooting Charlene a piercing look, she replied to Dylan. "That will be fine. Where should I meet you?"

"How about I pick you up and we can go——"

"Please don't say Mama's Place."

He laughed. "I was actually going to say out for seafood. I know a place that has amazing lobster rolls and the view isn't bad either. That is, if you don't mind a bit of a drive."

She wasn't driving, so it didn't matter. "Dylan, I'd be happy with something simple, like pizza or a burger."

"Good, we can do that tomorrow night. Tonight I'm craving lobster."

Tomorrow? They'd need to discuss that, but maybe after dinner.

"I'll see you at six." She ended the call and then turned back to Charlene, who looked mighty proud of herself. "Not one word, do you hear me?"

Charlene placed her fingers across her lips then burst out laughing, holding her ribs and practically falling off the couch.

And this is who I call a friend. Great.

Dylan hadn't expected her call, but was glad she had. It broke up the tension between him and his father. They were sitting in Dylan's office half staring at each other and waiting for the bomb to drop. It might as well be now.

"Dad, I need to ask you something. Something about Granddad."

"I didn't think you called me over here to talk business."

"In a way, it might be. Is there anything about Granddad that you didn't tell us?"

His father looked away for a minute, then turned back. "There's a lot about this family that has never been talked about. If you ask me, it should remain that way."

"Secrets aren't always a good thing. Actually, they always come out, but usually when you least want them to." Dylan knew that from experience when he was younger. Thankfully there wasn't anything that would permanently damage his reputation.

"These aren't mine to tell."

"Dad, I'd go to Granddad, but he's no longer with us."

He looked down and paused before saying, "Your grandfather was a tough man. Very tough. He demanded things be a certain way and when they weren't, let's just say, there was a price to pay."

"He was abusive?" Dylan could tell by his father's expression the answer was yes. *Fuck you, Granddad.* It explained a lot about how his father backed down. When raised in that type of environment, you either learned to fight back or how to duck and cover. Dylan was taught to respect his elders, but he'd have given his granddad an earful if he were still alive. "I'm sorry Dad. We never knew."

"I didn't want you to. That's why I made sure you were kept at a distance."

"You mean why you didn't bring any of us to work with you except for Charles?" He nodded. All this time, Dylan had

74

thought Charles was the favorite and that's why he was always with their father. Now he knew it was because the two of them had been protecting the younger ones. He probably owed Charles an apology, but those days had passed. Best thing he could do was make sure those mistakes don't happen again.

What Dylan didn't understand was why someone who seemed to have everything would be such an asshole. "Was Granddad always like that?"

"He had some...emotional problems which he didn't deal with very well. I'm going to say they stem from his child-hood. If you think your granddad wasn't a nice person, you should have seen your great-granddad."

"Do you think he hurt Granddad?"

"In ways that you couldn't imagine." He swore his father's eyes watered. "The Lawson family has been around for a long time. Its spotless reputation came at a high price. It's all a façade."

"Dad. Can you please tell me what you know?"

He looked at Dylan and asked, "Is it really that important? They are all dead now."

"It is if someone is out looking for answers."

"You?"

"No. Someone else," Dylan replied.

His father peered at him. "Henderson?"

That meant his father did know more than he wanted to say. But if he thought it could stay hidden forever, he just got the shock that it hadn't. "Yes. We have no proof it was Brice Henderson, but a woman on his staff was digging into our legacy. She uncovered something, and we don't know if it's true. Did Granddad have a...sister?"

It was the question they had all wanted to ask, but were hoping wasn't true.

"He did. Audrey."

"What happened to her?" Dylan asked.

His father snorted. "What the newspapers say, or the truth?"

"Both."

"The newspapers said Audrey was kidnapped from the home and never seen again. The truth was so much uglier than that."

Dylan wasn't sure how it could be, but he was about to learn. He wasn't going to be forceful with his father. Not ever again, not knowing what he'd been put through by his own father. "Tell me please. I need to know."

"Audrey was unstable. She also was very cruel to my father. My understanding was, she put him in the hospital with injuries more than once. The last time sent your great-granddad over the edge. He had Audrey taken away and I guess put in some type of institution."

That wasn't exactly what had happened, but his father didn't need to know Audrey was actually left all alone on a dirt road in the middle of nowhere. If it hadn't been for some stranger on a country drive, she might not have survived. But Audrey didn't know where she had come from or how she'd gotten there. They must have drugged her or something. That's why Audrey never reached out to her real family just a few states away. Back then, it wasn't like there was national news blaring every day on the TV. If you picked up something on the radio, you were doing well. And this wasn't as important as the end of World War Two. At least to most people. "Dad, does this mean that the story about Audrey marrying a Henderson is true?"

"It is. And your great-granddad and granddad both knew. That's why Lawson Steel was never allowed to do any business with them."

Dylan absorbed what he was being told. There were still so many questions, but right now, he only had one more. "Do they know?"

"The Hendersons?" he asked. Dylan nodded. "Not that I'm aware of. Audrey was a very...sick woman. There was a lot of speculation about how she even got Henderson to marry her in the first place. Let's just say, she was capable of some very unspeakable things. I asked my father what they were, but he wouldn't say. He said Audrey made him and my grandfather look like saints. Honestly Dylan, I don't want to know."

He got it. His father was getting older and at this point, that kind of shit was just going to add a stress that no one needed. That didn't mean Dylan didn't want to know it all. The Hendersons were his blood relations. Audrey was his great aunt. What he wasn't sure of was, how much of this did the Hendersons already know? Or was this their dirty little secret that they had kept hidden all these years too?

"Dad, I don't know what I'm going to do with this information yet, but I think it's something the others need to know." Dylan was speaking out of his own feelings on the topic. He already knew Gareth would agree. The others, well he wasn't sure. Charles probably was too much in a happy zone to want to hear this shit. That was a good thing. It'd give Dylan time to do more fact finding.

"Do as you wish with it. Just please, don't tell me what you learn."

"We won't Dad. And I promise, this won't go anywhere it doesn't need to." That meant the fewer people who knew, the better. But he was going to have a long talk with Gareth tomorrow. It might be time for them to take a trip to Boston. Sitting down with Brice Henderson will determine the next course of action.

Damn. Figures we have to be related to people with a reputation for always getting what they want. Must be in the genes.

He couldn't let their time together end on such a heavy note, so when they were finished with their deep conversation, Dylan decided to accompany his father back to visit with Penelope. Unfortunately, that took longer than he anticipated, and they weren't the only company there either.

"I don't have long, but I wanted to check on my little niece," Dylan said.

"And favorite sister-in-law," Rosslyn teased.

"Of course. But I really only have a few minutes," Dylan replied.

"Sounds like you have a hot date or something. Could it be that waitress from Mama's Place?" Gareth joked.

Rosslyn's eyes lit up. "Oh that would be wonderful. I'd love it if Penelope had someone close in age to grow up with."

What the fuck! How did it get from a date to a baby? Oh that would be a woman's way of thinking. Very dangerous. Many men had fallen into that trap, his brother Charles was one of them. She might be one, but that was enough to take down a room of men, especially with her newly acquired cohort, Penelope. Dylan knew it was time to get his ass out of there before Rosslyn was planning a wedding that wasn't ever going to happen.

Ignoring Rosslyn's comment he turned back to Gareth. "Sorry to disappoint you, but not everything revolves around women, Gareth." Dylan wasn't about to tell any of them that Gareth was right. Gareth already had a big enough ego and Rosslyn needed to focus on the baby, not on his love life. "But I do need to talk to you in the morning. My office at eight?"

"Damn. What happened to a nine-to-five job?"

Dylan laughed. "Then I suggest you get to bed early, because we have work to do." He walked over, kissed Rosslyn on the forehead and said, "She's beautiful just like her mother."

Charles said, "I couldn't agree with you more."

Rosslyn smiled, holding Penelope just a tad closer. "Come back any time, Dylan. You're always welcome."

Dylan knew that, but it was nice hearing it anyway. When he got into his car, he knew he was cutting it close to pick up Sofia on time. After his meeting with his father, his appetite was gone, but he couldn't cancel on her, not on their first date. Sofia was already resistant to being with him. That would be just enough to make her question this. So, he opted to send her a quick text letting her know he was on his way, then increased his speed. He might not be hungry, but he was looking forward to her company.

She must have been watching for him, because as soon as his Austin Healy pulled up, she came out. "I guess you're hungry," he said.

"I didn't want you to have to come up to the fourth floor for no reason."

"Fourth floor?"

She smiled. "You get used to it."

"I take it that means no elevator," he stated.

"Keeps me in shape. But really, it's not that bad. Unless it was laundry day, or I went food shopping. Then it sucks, and that is putting it lightly. You know, if you were busy, we didn't have to go out tonight."

"Are you trying to get out of it?" he asked.

"No. But I understand if something came up and plans needed to change," she said.

"That's good to know for the future, but I was just tied up

with my new niece. She's something else. I guess Sal lost track of time too when visiting earlier."

"I heard all about it from my mother. Boy, was she pissed at him. I don't think he'll shut his phone off for a month." Sofia chuckled. "At least that lets me off the hook for a while."

Dylan reached over and grabbed hold of her hand. "Does that mean we don't have to worry about any interruptions tonight?"

Sofia laughed. "We're not that lucky, but one could only hope. So where are you stealing me off to?"

"That's a secret. Why don't you sit back and relax? We have a drive ahead of us. But trust me, it'll be worth it."

"I'm sure it will," Sofia said as she settled back into the seat.

He wasn't sure what tonight was going to bring, but he knew one thing it wouldn't: *anything more than a kiss goodnight.* He was already playing with fire; it wouldn't take much more before he didn't give a fuck who didn't want them together. But since he wasn't looking for anything long term, it was his job to make sure he didn't cross any line that either of them would regret.

6

He had been right: the drive, although nice, was more than an hour. But the food was definitely worth it.

"How did you find this place?" Sofia asked.

"When I first got my license, I used to play this game. I'd drive to see if I could get lost, then see if I could find my way back."

"Sounds like fun. And you found this back then?"

He shook his head. "Don't laugh, but as I got older, the game changed. What can I say? I like a Sunday drive to nowhere."

"That's funny, since the name of the restaurant is 'In The Middle Of Nowhere'."

"I wasn't sure if you liked the ride or not. You got awful quiet for a bit," Dylan added.

She laughed. "I'm not sure if you noticed, but I was questioning where you were taking me. For a while there, this ride got a bit...scary. All the twists and turns, then the lack of streetlights kind of had the...horror-movie feel. Those dates *never* ended well."

Dylan choked on his drink and said, "I've been out on some bad dates, but nothing that extreme. I promise, no one is going to jump out of the woods with a chainsaw."

"That's always what you think right before it happens," she teased. "How will you explain that to Sal?"

Dylan shrugged. "It's not Sal that scares me. Or the guy with the chainsaw. Your mother, on the other hand, I think she'd skin me alive."

Sofia winked. "A wise man, I see. Don't you dare tell her I told you this, but her bark is much worse than her bite."

"If you don't mind, I'm not going to test that. I have a feeling you're bluffing."

Sofia laughed. "It's possible. So you'd better make sure I make it home safe and sound."

Dylan looked at her, no joking, and said, "I'd never let anyone hurt you Sofia."

The light, playful mood had changed. She missed it slightly, but it felt nice knowing that Dylan would protect her if needed. Sofia had been out on a few dates recently that were all about the guy and left her feeling like she'd probably have to fend for herself in a crisis. *Guess this is what it's like to be with a real man.*

Giving him a small, gracious smile, she said, "Thank you Dylan. Hopefully your services won't ever be required."

The waitress came over and asked, "Is there anything else you need? We'll be closing in a few minutes."

Sofia shook her head then looked at the clock. It was almost eleven. "We've been sitting here for hours."

"Guess my company doesn't suck," Dylan teased.

Sofia shrugged. "On a scale of one to ten, I'd give you a…strong eight."

"Eight?" he asked as they walked to the car.

"I hate to bring it up, but when you suggested we split a piece of death-by-chocolate cake, I believe you ate more than half." His tone was so serious that it sounded believable.

As he opened the car door for her, he asked, "Is there anything I can do to make it up to you?"

He was standing so close that she couldn't slip into the passenger's seat. Playfully she asked, "What are you offering?"

Dylan leaned over so he was only inches from her. She licked her lips in anticipation of his. But he didn't move any closer. Her chest heaved, as though she couldn't breathe. *Damn it.* Getting up on her tippy toes, Sofia wrapped her arms around his neck and pulled him to her. The kiss wasn't like the first. This one was hot and fierce. Lips clashing and tongues seeking. She felt his arms around her waist, pulling her up high against him. Her feet no longer on the ground, she was already soaring high on desire.

Sofia had never felt such a strong want building with just a kiss. If it hadn't been for a horn blaring, and a teenager shouting 'go for it,' they probably wouldn't have stopped.

Stammering, she said, "I think...you're a...strong nine...now."

Dylan laughed as he let her go. "I'll have to work harder tomorrow."

Slipping into the seat, she wasn't sure she could actually handle being around if it got any better. The raw passion that threatened to explode was stronger than anything she'd experienced. It excited and scared her. But no matter what, she looked forward to what tomorrow was going to bring.

Dylan didn't want the night to end, but she had been right,

morning was coming quick and she needed to work. That didn't mean he was going to get any sleep. Between his meeting with his father and then being out with Sofia, he was fucking wound up. Since Gareth wasn't in the mood for meeting bright and early, it only made sense to do it now.

Looking across the table, Dylan questioned that decision. Gareth was up, but he was more interested in the beer he was drinking than anything Dylan had to say.

"This was a waste of time," Dylan snarled.

Gareth said, "Not totally."

"Please tell me how it wasn't?"

Gareth raised his glass and said, "We're not in the office discussing this."

"We're not discussing anything. I thought you wanted to be involved in this." It was the impression he'd gotten several days ago. Things seemed to have changed.

"I do. And from what you said, you have your answer. Audrey Lawson married Clint Henderson. None of this is going to change how we do business going forward. Hell, if anything, it should make things easier. We no longer need to worry about why Granddad forbade us from doing business with them. So what? They're our cousins. Doesn't change anything as far as I'm concerned."

"That's because you weren't there when Dad was talking. This wasn't just Aunt Audrey running away and getting hitched. There's a lot more to it. And really, Granddad might have been an abusive asshole to Dad, but I think he was dealing with a lot of shit himself. Shit Gareth, it seems like violence was how our family handled everything." Dylan ran his hand through his hair. Right now, being a Lawson almost made him sick. "Think about it, Gareth. Our great-granddad got rid of his child and never looked back."

"I'm trying *not* to think about it, Dylan. When I do, I get pissed off. You hear about shit like this happening in other families, but I never expected it to be ours," Gareth said, before guzzling down the rest of his beer.

"I can't help but think about Maxwell Grayson," Dylan said.

"What the hell does he have to do with anything?"

Dylan shrugged. "We went after him for all the horrendous things he'd done, several illegal. Who are we to have done that? Hell Gareth, we're just as bad, if not worse."

Gareth slammed down his empty glass on the table. "Don't you ever put us in the same category as Maxwell or our grandparents. We're *none* of those things."

"Maybe not. But that's our gene pool. Our legacy. How the hell do we hold our heads up and proudly say we are Lawsons now?"

"I guess we don't look back, and keep moving forward like we've been doing? But that doesn't seem to be what you want to do."

Dylan shook his head. "I'm going to reach out to Brice Henderson."

"I want to tell you what a huge mistake you're making, but I've thought about doing that myself."

"What's stopping you?" Dylan asked.

"I guess I'm afraid I'll find out more than I want to know. This already sucks Dylan. Are you sure you're ready for the rest?"

Dylan wasn't sure how much worse it could get. Things were pretty fucked up already. "What's worse? Us finding out, or the Hendersons using it against us?"

Gareth nodded. "They're not our competitor, but if they ever became one, it would be leverage not in our favor."

"Exactly. I think it'd be good to know if they would stand by us or against us too if the truth ever got out. We might be family, but one thing I've learned, blood isn't as thick as the dollar sign." If it had been, Rosslyn's parents wouldn't have been put through hell. Of course, if Rosslyn had been around Maxwell, it was possible she might not be the sweet person she was today. "Gareth, do you think Aunt Audrey straightened out after what our great-granddad did to her?"

"You mean did she stop her sadistic ways?" Gareth asked. Dylan nodded. "Guess that's something only a Henderson could answer. If they're anything like us, they're good about keeping their dirt hidden. But I can't see how what our great-granddad did to her would've made things any better. If anything, I'd think it amplified it."

"Meaning their grandmother might have been abusive to their father as well?"

"It's tough. We can only speculate," Gareth said.

"And that's why I need to meet with Brice. He had our family looked into for a reason. I need to know why." *What was he looking for?*

"Then I guess we'd better get home and get some sleep, because I'm not letting you go meet with them on your own."

"What do you think they'll do?" Dylan asked.

"I'm not sure. Not sure about a lot of things anymore."

Dylan felt the exact same way. For years he'd wanted to run Lawson Steel. Now even the name left a bitter taste in his mouth. Would the others feel the same way once they learned the truth?

Should we even tell them? He knew the answer. It was just a matter of when and how. Hopefully it wasn't going to cause a ripple effect throughout them. *I guess what we learn from Brice will determine that.*

"I'll pick you up at eight and we can head to Boston," Dylan said.

"Make it ten. We don't have an appointment with him anyway. And it's probably best to keep it that way."

"And you think he'll see us why?" Dylan asked.

"Because we're Lawsons."

And Brice probably has questions too.

7

There was nothing wrong with Dylan having to cancel the dinner date. It wasn't like they were really dating, anyway. After the morning she was having at the restaurant and little sleep, she really was looking forward to going back to her apartment and crashing. Besides, she needed to look over the script. Rehearsals started next week, and she was far from ready.

Sofia thought about asking Charlene to read through the lines with her, but she'd just pester for details Sofia wasn't ready to share. She was still trying to figure out what was with that kiss.

It wasn't like her to be so...forward. If Dylan wanted to kiss her, then fine. If he didn't, so what? But actually pulling him down to her and taking what she wanted was out of character. Maybe Charlene was rubbing off on her. Whatever it was, she hoped it didn't give Dylan the wrong impression. Yes, she liked him. But she wasn't the 'take me home, hop in bed' type. And she wasn't even looking for a relationship now, either. Where would she squeeze in dating? Between work and the show, she'd be lucky if she could find any time for herself, never mind another person.

That didn't mean she could brush away the thoughts of last night. That kiss had to be what kicked off her steamy dreams last night. She woke up in a dead sweat, panting so hard, that she'd have sworn that orgasm was real. *That he was real.*

But a wet dream was only a sign that she was sexually frustrated, and nothing more. Her intense reaction to his kiss and touch was because of the same. Now, if she were Charlene, she'd have her head in the clouds, thinking of how they were destined to find each other, and the sexual chemistry was their souls connecting, causing a spark.

It was funny, because she never would've thought Charlene would fall for all that mushy stuff. If anything, Charlene was the wild one who used to think that if you want something, you go for it, and Sofia used to be the hopeless romantic. Over the years, something had changed that. Maybe it was being overworked or seeing so many relationships fall apart that had crushed it for her. But romance was for fairytales and dreamers. She was chasing something bigger than both.

Pouring herself a glass of pink lemonade, she settled down to start reading. Most of the lines had nothing to do with her, but the director said everyone should know it. *You never know when something might happen and you'll be asked to fill in.* But her character didn't even have a name, just 'beggar number three.' There was a long way to go before she had to worry, or hope, to get some larger role. At least she had some lines to say and was in the chorus for a few songs. More like humming, but she was still on the stage. *And I'm being paid too.*

Of course, her wage didn't even equate to what she made in a day at the restaurant. But this wasn't about money. At least, not right now it wasn't. She needed to be noticed, get her name out there. *And not as beggar number three, either.*

Closing her eyes, she laid back on the couch for a minute and could almost see her name, Sofia Marciano, lit up in lights with gold stars on both ends. Hordes of people would be waiting in long lines to get in to see her. But they were all strangers. No one looked familiar. Was that the price she was going to pay for fame and fortune? It was her dream, in a way. But before, it hadn't mattered to her who was there. She wanted away from this mundane life. Things were changing and she...kind of liked her life right now.

The problem was, starting Monday, it was changing again and she wouldn't have time for Dylan or Charlene or any of her family and friends. Not if she truly wanted to make a good impression on the director. Not only did she need to be there every night, but on time and ready to shine. The way she felt right now, she had no luster. Lust yes, but luster no.

Sofia realized that time was flying by and she hadn't done anything but lie back and think of what she wanted. Why couldn't she focus? Getting up, she decided maybe a coffee would help. She poured her lemonade down the sink drain and pressed start on her coffee pot. It was set to go off in the morning, but she could always set up another pot before bed. Sadly, bed was exactly where she wanted to be right now.

The aroma of the fresh brew definitely was working. Her eyes opened wide and she was finally ready to start. Of course the knock on the door, three taps and a pause before the last, meant Charlene was stopping in unannounced. Opening the door, she said, "Did you smell it on your way up?"

Having a friend live on the floor above was really handy

most of the time. Other times, it was a nuisance. Sofia wasn't sure yet which this was.

"You do make amazing coffee, but that's not why I'm here." Charlene walked over to the couch and flopped down. "You'll never believe what happened."

Sofia poured Charlene a cup, walked over, and sat down. "Try me," she said as she handed her the mug.

Charlene took one sip then smiled. "This is good." But it wasn't long before the caffeine jolt kicked in. "Okay, back to what happened. I was on my way to work this morning and this pickup truck rammed into the back of my car."

Sofia reached out and asked, "Are you okay?"

Charlene waved her hand. "Yeah. I'm fine. So this guy hits my car. I get out all pissed off at him and ready to read him the riot act. But when he gets out, well, let's just say I was left speechless."

Still concerned, Sofia asked, "Why? Was he hurt?"

"No. Trust me, there was absolutely *nothing* wrong with this guy. He was…wow. About six foot six and rugged, with a cowboy hat on and the sweetest blue eyes you've ever seen."

"Charlene, focus. What about the accident?" Sofia said, prodding Charlene back to this planet.

She took another sip of coffee. "Well, it seems he was pulling his horse trailer. There is this woman in Massachusetts who's rescuing two horses from being slaughtered. Imagine that? They were healthy-looking and young, and so friendly, and they were just going to destroy them. How sad is that?"

She felt for the animals, but still had no idea where Charlene was going with this conversation. "Were the horses okay?"

"Yes, they are fine too."

"Good. You're okay. The cowboy is okay and the horses are fine. That's great." *Now drink your coffee and go so I can study.*

"Well you didn't let me finish. His brakes let go so his truck needed to be fixed. Well, I couldn't just leave him there in a strange town with no place to go. So I brought him to Mama's Place for a late lunch. By the way, Emily is good, but she's not you."

"Thanks."

"Well, the mechanic said the truck will be ready shortly."

"Great. And they can be on their way to their new home." Charlene was good at making a short story long.

"Yup, and I'm going for the ride." Charlene beamed.

Sofia blinked several times, as though it might help her hear something else, something logical. "You're doing what?"

"He asked me if I wanted to tag along. I said yes."

Sofia got up off the couch and paced the floor before she turned back and said firmly, "You're crazy. You can't go anywhere with this guy. You just met him this morning. How do you know he's not a murderer or something?"

"Sofia, he helps horses. How can someone like that be a bad person?"

She threw her hands up in the air. In a more forceful voice, she asked, "Have you ever watched the news? Seen a horror movie? They always look nice until they're not. You can't go."

Charlene got up slowly and said, "Listen *mom,* I'm old enough to make my own decisions. And besides, your mother liked him."

"My mother said you should go?" Sofia asked.

Charlene replied, "I didn't ask. But she said he seemed like a very nice young man. Hell Sofia, I haven't met anyone like him in a long time. Everyone here is…the same. He's so…different. What the hell do I have to lose?"

"Your life," she snapped.

"Now who's being overdramatic? I promise, nothing is going to happen to me. It's only for the weekend. I'll be back Sunday night."

"Charlene, you're really going to do this, aren't you?" Charlene nodded. Sofia knew there was no talking her out of it. "Then I want you to promise me to text me all his information."

"Got it. And I'll even check in every few hours if you want."

"Okay." It was better than nothing.

"I've got to go. I'm meeting him at the garage in an hour and I need to shower and pack." Charlene gave Sofia a hug and added, "Try to have some fun yourself while I'm gone. I hate thinking of you sitting in this apartment, bored."

I won't be. I'll be praying that you're safe. "I'll be studying. Now don't forget, I want his name and the license plate, and maybe a picture too."

"Sure, and I'll ask his blood type as well," Charlene joked.

Sofia wasn't laughing. She really was going to worry the entire time. But one good thing about having a brother on the police department, once she had the info from Charlene, she could find out if the guy really was a nice one or not. *Please be what you seem to be. She's my best friend and I couldn't stand it if anything happened.*

Charlene left the apartment and Sofia stood there motionless. Things were changing, and right now, she didn't like it at all. Studying and being prepared for Monday weren't going to happen. *What a way to start my weekend.*

. . .

Dylan pulled up in front of the Henderson building and said, "You ready for this?"

Gareth asked, "Are you worried?" Dylan nodded. Gareth said, "We can turn around and go home. No one knows we're here. No harm done so far."

He was tempted to do just that. "And then we're back where we started. Not a place I want to be."

"Then park this thing and let's go inside before they have security come out and ask us to move."

Dylan put it in park and shut off the engine. Sure enough, someone was approaching. "Do you have an appointment?" he asked.

Dylan shook his head. "No, but we're here to see Brice Henderson."

"Not without an appointment," the security guard stated.

Gareth pulled out a business card and said, "Call him and tell him the Lawsons from New York are here."

The guard looked at the card then at the two of them. He spoke into a mic that was attached to his shoulder. "I have two men here to see Brice. They don't have appointments. Their last name is Lawson. They said they're from New York."

There was a delay, and the guy just stood there blocking their entrance. It was kind of funny, because neither of them was going to rush the place. If Brice wouldn't see them, then it didn't matter. It meant he wasn't going to give them any valuable information anyway.

A moment later the guard said firmly, "Come with me."

Dylan looked at Gareth as though this had to be a joke. This guy obviously had no idea who they were. Then again, it was possible Brice didn't either. They were soon to find out. The guard escorted them up a private elevator but stood with his chest puffed out, as though it intimidated either of them. They weren't impressed. They were from New York and used to dealing with people a hell of a lot scarier than that guard.

When they got out they were met by an older woman with a very cheery disposition. "Hello. I'm Nancy. Brice is just finishing up with a meeting but he'd like to see you both right after. Would you mind waiting a few minutes?"

"Not at all," Gareth said.

"Wonderful. I can show you to a private conference room, or you can wait here by my desk. Whichever you prefer."

"Here will be fine," Dylan said.

"And how about coffee?" Nancy asked. They both shook their head. "Please let me know if you change your mind. I do make the best cup in Boston. Don't tell his wife Lena that. She thinks hers tops mine."

Dylan hadn't thought about Brice's family when he had decided to come. It was a complication that he'd intentionally avoided thinking about. But as this next generation was being born, like Penelope, it made Dylan want to tighten up all those loose ends that others had created. *No more surprises. No more lies.*

They didn't need to wait very long and when the door opened, Dylan recognized the man leaving the office. It was the youngest Henderson, Dean. Dylan wondered if they had been discussing what to say or not to them. It was a question Dylan planned on asking.

Once Dean was out of earshot, Brice walked over and said, "Why don't you two come into my office where we can talk in private."

They followed him in and took the two high-back leather seats across from Brice's desk. "You seem to have been expecting us," Dylan said.

"I was hoping this day wouldn't come. Please pardon me if that sounds…rude. But under the circumstances, I'm sure you agree," Brice stated as he took his seat.

More than you know. "Should we get right to the point?" Brice nodded. "I'm sure you know who we are. I'm Dylan and this is Gareth."

"I'm Brice and that was Dean who I was meeting with earlier."

"Is he aware of why we're here?" Gareth asked.

"I'm not even sure he knows who you are. I've kept what I know quiet. Actually, I was hoping that this day would never come. It seems Roger, an associate of mine, didn't cover the tracks as well as we had hoped."

Dylan asked, "You mean from Gia, the woman who you had investigate us?"

Brice replied, "That wasn't how it started."

Gareth said, "Then enlighten us."

"My father wasn't what you would call a nice person. I'm not even sure they have created a word that could describe his sick demented mind or actions. Some people should never be born. He's one of them," Brice snarled out. Dylan could see the disgust in his eyes as Brice spoke about his father. "It's not something any of us are proud of, but we can't change our past. Over the years I learned that it's best to be proactive when it comes to my father's secrets. None of them ever turned out to be good. So, when I found a photo of a young girl and small boy, I had Roger do some research. We weren't looking into *your* family; I was having him look into mine."

"And you found the connection, Aunt Audrey," Gareth stated.

"My grandmother," Brice replied.

"Do you know what my great-grandfather did to her?" Dylan asked.

"Not everything. I heard that he faked her disappearance and she ended up here. I also know there are some questions regarding my grandfather's first wife," Brice said.

"Audrey was working in the mill that my grandfather owned. He was a tough bastard who didn't treat his workers nicely. It was all about making himself richer. But there was one worker who he paid special attention to."

Dylan snarled, "Audrey."

"Yes. But my grandfather was married. His wife was murdered," Brice said.

Gareth asked, "You think your grandfather did it?"

He shook his head. "No. He had an alibi. I believe it was Audrey, my grandmother. She always got what she wanted, and if that was my grandfather, she'd have made sure Gloria was out of the way."

"Damn. That's fucked up," Gareth said, then added, "No disrespect, 'cause that's our family too."

"Trust me, I have no love for my grandmother or my father. The world is a better place without either of them."

"I think we agree that there was quite a bit of damage done by one disturbed young girl," Gareth said.

Dylan added, "Where does the blame stop? With our great-granddad? He's the one who didn't help her."

"It was a different time back then, Dylan. No one understood someone like Audrey. The only thing to do was to pretend she never existed. Unfortunately, she had my father and passed along her abusive ways to him," Brice said. "I feel for anyone directly affected by her actions."

"Like our granddad. Audrey had abused him so much that he did the same to our father." Dylan ran his hand through his hair. "I have no idea how our father didn't do the same to us."

"There are things, Dylan, that we're never going to know. It was a long time ago. We could keep digging, but what good will it do? None of us can change it. All we can do is try not to be anything like them," Brice said.

Dylan peered at him long and hard. Was he sharing everything he knew? There seemed to be more. "What aren't you telling us Brice?"

"You don't want to know," he replied.

"We're here for a reason," Gareth said.

Brice let out a heavy sigh. "There were things my father did, that are very disturbing. But what he did was recruit some other wealthy bastard to help him do his dirty work."

"Does this have to do with why you and your family are spending billions of dollars in Tabiq?" Gareth asked.

Brice arched a brow. "You have done your homework."

"We might be related, but that doesn't mean we trust you," Gareth added.

"Nor I you," Brice replied. "But to answer your question, yes, the Tabiq project has everything to do with my father. It might be too late for some, but it's our mission to break the pattern."

"And this has what to do with us?" Dylan asked.

"Your dear old granddad was one of the people my father seemed to connect with on a regular basis. I don't think my father had a clue he was his uncle. At that time, my father only saw someone who hated women as much as he did. What neither of them realized, it was the same woman who had brought that hatred upon them."

Dylan said, "One woman, two families, and a hell of a lot of—"

"Cruelty," Brice said.

"And yet, we all seem, would 'normal' be too strong of a word?" Gareth asked.

Brice and Dylan both nodded. "I don't know about the

Lawsons, but for the Hendersons, it's always in the back of our minds. A fear of finding out we're no better. But the more I learn about them, the more I know we're nothing like them."

"God I hope not." Dylan turned to Gareth and asked, "Is there anything else you want to know?"

"Yes. Charles mentioned that years ago there was a business deal on the table between you and him. Something changed. What was it?"

"I'm not sure. Everything was in order. Asher Barrington and I were in the process of building a factory overseas. But then suddenly, the communication ended and the contract didn't go through. We went with someone else," Brice said.

"So you had no idea back then who we were? That we're your cousins?" Gareth asked.

"No. If I did, I'm not sure it would've changed anything. Not then, at least. My father was still alive and I kept my distance from him as much as possible. We all did," Brice said. "It actually was his death that brought us back together. If he were still alive…well, let's just say I wouldn't be a father now."

"I'm sure your mother had a positive influence on you," Dylan said.

"That's a story for another time," Brice said. "But we did have a strong female influence. Asher and I have known each other a long time. His mother Sophie must've realized that there were a few things lacking in our home and I'm not talking about money. We had an abundance of that, which I guess was supposed to make up for everything else. It didn't. Kindness, love, compassion were forbidden whether it be towards each other, or outsiders. Any sign of it, came with a punishment. But Sophie had an open door policy and we were always welcome. Because of her, we knew what a normal family looked like. If it wasn't for her, God knows what type of men we'd have turned out to be. Not saying we're saints, but we're nothing even close to what our father James was. It's a name I still have trouble saying."

Brice didn't even try to hide his dislike, maybe hatred, for his father. Some wounds don't heal even after time. "Then I guess we got lucky, because our mother was that for us," Dylan replied. "If it weren't for her, I'm not sure what my father would've been. Even now, she is what keeps him... rooted." *Us on the other hand, no one tells us what to do. Well Charles isn't so lucky any more.*

"So where do we go from here?" Gareth asked. "Do we tell the others that our family tree just got a whole lot bigger? There are six of you, right?"

Brice laughed. "Once again, that story is for another time. But to answer your question, I'm not sure how to present this to everyone. We definitely don't want this getting out of control and the media learning of our connection."

"You mean what really happened to Aunt Audrey?" Dylan asked.

"Yes. That will have them taking a closer look into both our families. There are things my father and your granddad did that we don't want our children to ever know, never mind the rest of the world. It wouldn't matter who or what we are doing now, we'd be the ones answering for their actions."

Dylan nodded. "So continue with this charade and don't acknowledge we're family."

"I wish there were another way," Brice said. "But know that I'm here if you need me."

"Vice versa," Gareth said.

Dylan got up and before leaving he asked, "And you trust this Roger person and Gia?"

"They are like family to me. Hendersons watch out for each other. I'd like to think that we can learn to trust each other as well," Brice said.

Trust. That was a funny word when it seemed so much of their family history was based around lies. There was something else that bound them all together besides Audrey. They were all victims, in one way or another. *Not a club any of us want to be part of.*

"I guess time will tell," Dylan said before leaving the office.

Gareth said as they got into Dylan's car, "That went better than I thought."

Dylan turned to him and said, "You obviously weren't in the same room as I was, because that was a shit show. All I know is, we got some fucked-up genes."

"Yup, but after listening to Brice, it makes me glad to be a Lawson. Sounds like their father James is a hell of a lot more fucked up than our father," Gareth added.

Dylan laughed as he pulled the car into traffic. "Great. We're comparing who's more fucked up, and not which one isn't. Not sure that makes us the winners."

"It's all how you look at things, Dylan. Trust me, I have a feeling we are. But I have to admit, I want to know what the hell happened in Tabiq."

"Gareth, if our granddad was involved, it can't be good. Do you really want to know?" Dylan couldn't believe that had come out of his mouth. Not after he was the one who'd pushed this meeting in the first place.

"Can't fix it if we don't know what's broke," Gareth replied.

And 'broken' was exactly how Dylan saw both sides of the family. Two pieces that never should've been joined together. *Thanks, Great-granddad. You really did a royally fucked-up job at keeping your legacy going. I really hope there's nothing else you did that we don't know about because if so, I'm changing my name.*

8

Her phone vibrated but she was with a customer, so she couldn't answer it. It was crazy busy on Saturday mornings, and Sunday was even worse. Whoever it was would need to leave a message. Since Charlene had held to her promise and had been texting or calling most of the night, it was probably her with another update, or photo of the horses. Sofia was still worried, but Charlene really looked like she was enjoying herself. There was even one picture of her cleaning out the back of the horse trailer. Shoveling poop wasn't something Sofia ever thought she'd see Charlene do. *She really must like this guy.*

It wouldn't have been so bad last night, but it sucked getting all these messages about how much fun it all was while she was stuck home alone. Sofia understood that something came up and Dylan had to cancel. It probably was better that way. The last thing she wanted was to get used to seeing him and then have it end. She already enjoyed being with him too much.

The drive back from dinner had been so nice. She wasn't sure how the time flew by so quickly, but it hadn't seemed like an hour drive. He let her go on and on about her dream and what she was working on. She even told him about the part in the play, although small, and he seemed impressed. Maybe she saw what she wanted, but as far as dates go, that night had been nearly perfect.

The only thing she'd change is the kiss goodnight. It was...too brief. Then again, they'd been sitting in his car, because she'd told him it was unnecessary to walk her up four flights of stairs for nothing. That statement was as good as telling Dylan, "Don't bother, because you're getting shot down." That wasn't how she'd meant it. Of course, she wasn't about to sleep with the guy, but some kissing and snuggling on the couch wouldn't have been so bad. *And oh, that man can kiss. Starts sweet and ends spicy.*

"Excuse me miss, but did you get our order right?"

Sofia looked down at the pad and she had written eggs over easy. She was positive there was more than that, since there were two people at the table. She blushed with embarrassment, as she'd never daydreamed like that before in front of a customer. It was understandable, based on how he made her feel, but still totally unacceptable.

"I'm so sorry. Could you please repeat it one more time?"

Although the woman smiled, the gentleman she was with wasn't cutting her any slack. "I have no faith we're going to get what we order anyway. She's not even paying attention."

"I'm very sorry. I can guarantee you that your food will be exactly as you order it," Sofia said.

"And on the house too," her mama chimed in from behind.

Oh shit. It was bad enough when a customer noticed, but her mother was going to chew her butt out.

The man said, "Then let me give you my order. I'll have the steak and eggs, steak done medium well and the eggs poached on wheat toast with extra butter. I want homefries and—"

"Honey, please. Look at her. She's in love. I remember that look in my eyes when we were first dating. I couldn't stop thinking about you at all." The woman smiled. "So please honey, give her a break. And be happy for her, because seeing her brings back some very special memories."

The man reached across the table and said, "I still feel the same way every time I think of you."

The woman choked up and said, "Oh, I love you so much. Now how about ordering for real?"

The man turned back and smiled. "We'll each have two poached egged on wheat toast and coffee. And I'm sorry about giving you a hard time."

Sofia wrote it down. "Thank you so much for being so understanding. I'll be right back with your food."

Although the customers let her off the hook, her mother followed her into the kitchen and waited until she gave her father the order. Preparing for what was coming, she turned around and said, "I know, Mama. I was wrong. It won't happen again."

Her mother didn't say a word about her screwing up the order. "Is it true? Are you in love?"

A strong like. Lust. Love, no. But he was definitely someone she could see herself with. At least, right now it seemed that way. "Mama, it's too early. We're still getting to know each other."

"What is there to know? He is a boy, you're a girl, you either like him or not."

Sofia bit her tongue to keep from laughing. There was so much more to making a relationship work, but in her mother's eyes, it was so simple. "Mama, this isn't the time. Customers are waiting."

"Let them wait," she replied. "You are my only daughter and I need to know."

It was wonderful that her mother was putting Sofia's feelings above all, but really, there was nothing to tell. At least, not that she could. The truth was very confusing, even for Sofia. *Gee Mama, we were only pretending to be dating, but I guess I really like the guy and that sucks because none of it is real. Or at least, I don't know what is and what isn't.*

"Mama, I like him." *A lot.* "He makes me laugh and listens to me talk about my dreams for my future."

"Ah. Good. I should have Papa sit down and talk to him about the restaurant too."

The restaurant? Ha. Sofia wanted to say that was not her dream, never had been. But the more concerning thing was her mother spreading rumors about her and Dylan. If Mama wanted to talk to Papa, it was going to be a serious conversation. It wasn't the time for that. Panic filled her. If Papa thought Dylan was 'the one,' then he'd want to have a sit-down, man-to-man talk. Papa was usually quiet, but she knew he wouldn't be then. Poor Dylan would be blindsided and for what? Being a friend to her? She couldn't let that happen. Sofia needed to speak up.

"Mama, please. Times are different now. People take things slow. Besides, I'm in no rush."

Maria huffed. "You're not getting any younger."

"Mama, there is no reason to be married and have children so young."

"You are already too old for that. You're almost thirty."

"I'm twenty-six," Sofia corrected.

"Exactly. The clock is ticking, Sofia, and you can't afford to waste time. I'm going to invite Dylan over for dinner and the five of us can talk."

Sofia wanted no such thing, but she couldn't figure out who the other person was. "Five?"

"Salvatore. He will want to talk to Dylan too." She turned around and grabbed two plates with the order already prepared. "Now go and do your job. Your father and I will handle the rest."

Sofia knew she should just come clean. It'd be so much easier than waiting. Once her mother reached out to Dylan, it would be out anyway. So what was holding her back? *Maybe I'll get lucky and a meteor will land on my apartment and I won't ever have to worry about any of it.* She looked one last time at her mother before leaving the kitchen. She seemed so…filled with joy. How could she break her heart?

As soon as this shift was over, Sofia was giving Dylan a call. Her acting skills better be strong, because she was going to need to convince Mama and Papa that she and Dylan were anything but a match for each other. It wasn't going to be easy, but really, she could think of this as one large stage and her chance to have the lead role. Of course, she didn't have a script, and the critic was her mother. *And no dress rehearsals, either.*

Carrying the dishes out to the dining area, she remembered there was someone else who needed to be on board with this as well. *Dylan Lawson, this was your bright idea, how are we going to fix it now?*

Although she should have been home studying for the play, it seemed like she was going to need to see Dylan. This could be handled over the phone, but the faster they nipped this in the bud, the better. One thing about the Marciano family, their excitement could get the better of them and things quickly got out of hand.

All this because of one stinking kiss that she couldn't stop thinking about. *And it was so worth it.*

.   .   .

Dylan had called her in the morning but hadn't left a message. It was Saturday, and his first thought was Sofia had opted to sleep in. Then after speaking to Charles, he stood corrected. Sofia worked seven days a week. It was no wonder she was exhausted. He actually felt bad about keeping her out so late on Thursday. At least a small part of him did. He enjoyed her company. If he didn't, he wouldn't have been with her.

But with everything else going on in her life, he was surprised to get a text from her asking if they could meet tonight. Of course, he agreed, but she hadn't given any indication as to why. His gut told him it wasn't because she missed him. Oddly enough, he did miss her.

There was no doubt there was a physical connection, and he found their conversations intriguing, but she wasn't his type. She was family oriented, whether she wanted to admit it or not. Sofia could tell him anything she wanted, but deep-rooted values were exactly what bound her to the restaurant. Not that Dylan didn't respect his parents, but even from a young age, he'd done what he wanted, not necessarily what was asked or expected of him.

He'd offered to help her so she could attempt to follow her dream, but he knew she never would. Not that she couldn't make it as an actress, it was very possible; she was amazing. Yet, she took 'honor thy mother and father' very seriously. Her talent took the backseat. Dylan wasn't sure if he respected or hated that about her. Either way, it showed him how different they were.

Nothing stood in Dylan's way when he wanted something. The more time they spent together, the more difficult it was becoming for him to know exactly what that was. At first, he was just helping Sal's kid sister. No big deal. It'd be a few weeks, then back to normal for them both.

Yet Sofia had to know she wasn't making it easy on him. Boldly kissing him like she had almost sent him over the edge. Holding back from taking it to the next level was getting harder each time he laid eyes on her. She was beautiful in the most natural way. At the restaurant, she didn't even wear any makeup. And when they went out, even then, only a touch.

It was so much more than just her stunning looks. He crossed paths with beautiful women every day in the city. But combine her looks with her spirit, and she was as unique as a de Vinci painting. Someone could try to replicate her ways, but you'd always know they weren't the real thing.

Even now, with all the distractions around Aunt Audrey and the Hendersons, he couldn't stop thinking about her. Dylan needed to let her know this was a mistake. He had to focus on his shit right now. It was yet another night when he could be accomplishing something, either at Lawson Steel or Grayson Corp., and instead he was about to knock on her door. He was here, because he wanted to be. That troubled him more.

A quick knock and she opened the door. Sofia was on her cell phone trying to calm someone down.

"It's okay. I can drive there now and pick you up. No. I don't want you taking a bus. You just stay right there and I'll come for you."

He watched Sofia as she walked around her apartment and started grabbing things and tossing them into her purse. Dylan wanted to ask who she was talking to, but it really wasn't any of his business. From the looks of it, if he'd gotten there a few minutes later, Sofia wouldn't have been home. Did this call have anything to do with her asking him here?

He'd need to be patient and wait to find out. Not one of his virtues. For Sofia, he'd make more of an effort. It was killing him, because he could tell by her body language, she was concerned about the other person on the phone.

"Please promise me you won't do anything stupid," Sofia said. "No, I'm not saying you *are* stupid. Just don't do anything rash. I'll be there in a few hours. I'll rent a car if I have to. Just wait for me," she ordered.

Dylan could eliminate a few people off the list. It wasn't her parents or Sal on the phone. He wished he could hear the voice to determine if it was a male or female on the other end, but Sofia wasn't standing still long enough for him to get close. Finally, she ended the call and turned to him.

"I'm really sorry, but I have to go," she blurted. Sofia grabbed her keys and headed for the door.

Dylan grabbed hold of her arm and said, "Sofia, I'm not sure you should be driving."

She looked down at his hand then up to face him. "Why?"

"You have only one sneaker on. Unless that was planned, I think you're a bit...distracted at the moment."

Sofia rolled her eyes and started looking through her purse. Sure enough, she pulled the other one out. "What the hell?" She walked over to the couch and started putting it on. "You might be right, but I have no choice, I have to go."

It'd be so easy just to let her leave, but the words came out anyway. "Go where?"

"Hudson, Massachusetts."

That was about a three- to four-hour drive, depending on traffic. With it being early on a Saturday night, it might not be too bad. "And what is there that can't wait a few minutes?" What he meant was *who*.

"Charlene. And she is hysterical. I could barely understand her, she was crying so much."

"Charlene? Is she…family?" As far as Dylan knew, it was just her and Sal.

"No. She's my best friend and she needs me," Sofia said, getting up and grabbing her purse again.

"And I think right now you could use a driver. Why don't I go with you?"

Sofia stopped. "That's nice and everything, but you don't understand. She's bawling her eyes out. You *don't* want to be in the car with her. She'll be rattling off stuff that might make you uncomfortable."

It sounded like hell to him, but he wasn't retracting his offer. "What makes me *uncomfortable,* is the thought of you doing this drive alone." She stood there, as though debating what to do. "Or you can ask your brother to go with you." Sofia shot him a warning look. He raised his hands. "Just putting it out there. You do have options. I believe I'm the best one, since I'm standing in front of you and my car is gassed up."

"You don't have to do this, you know."

"Well, since you asked me here, I figured this little road trip might give us time to talk as well." He wasn't sure about *what*.

"That's true, but we could talk on the phone while I drove there," Sofia retorted.

"And we could stand here all night debating what to do, while your friend is in distress. So are we going or not?" Dylan always won in debate class, and from the look on her face, he hadn't lost his touch.

"Fine, but I'm paying for gas and tolls," she said as she headed for the door.

He didn't bother replying. When they were in the car, she gave him the address and he punched it into his GPS. Once on the road, he turned to her and asked, "What happened to

Charlene?"

"Oh it's a long story."

"We have time. Actually, three hours and twenty-nine minutes, to be exact," he said, trying to lighten the mood. It didn't work.

"I told her not to go. Warned her it could be a mistake. But she kept sending me pictures and updates and she seemed to be happy."

That wasn't giving him much of anything. "This seems like the short version. Want to try again with a bit more detail?"

"That's the first time anyone ever told me to talk more," Sofia snorted. "Trust me, someday you'll regret saying those words."

I could listen to your voice for hours and never grow tired of it. And once she started telling him about Charlene, he realized that was being tested.

"You can't just meet a guy and then a few hours later, decide to travel with him."

"I'd have to agree. There are predators waiting to victimize someone." Dylan knew he didn't need to elaborate on that. It was all over social media every day. He felt for her friend but was damn glad it wasn't Sofia in that situation. *Hopefully she'd never be that foolish. So help me, I'd kill anyone who hurt her.*

"I guess she was so taken with his looks and charm that she only saw a fun adventure. But to me, nothing about that felt right. You'd think she'd listen to me, but nope. Off she went with him and his horses."

"They rode off on horses and made it all the way to Hudson in that short period?" Dylan knew he was missing something. That didn't make sense, even if they had lived in

Texas. Sofia explained how the two had met, during a little so-called fender bender.

"Now that I'm telling you the story, I know how lucky she is that it wasn't worst. All he did was get stinking drunk and make a move on her. But when he wouldn't take no for an answer, she made sure he would only be hitting the high notes for a while, if you know what I mean."

That he did. His balls tightened just thinking about it. "Good." *Not that it will teach him a lesson, but at least he won't mess with her.* "Did she call the police?"

Sofia shook her head. "She's embarrassed by the entire thing. All she wants to do is come home and forget about it."

Dylan said, "Maybe you can convince her to do otherwise." Sofia looked at him, wide eyed. "No man should lay a hand on a woman. I'm glad she handled it, but there is nothing wrong with filing a police report as well."

This wasn't something he'd ever normally say. He may have felt that way all along, but voice it? No. The change had to do with his Aunt Audrey. Something had set her off to be so violent, to hate men so much. Dylan hadn't asked the question because no one could possibly know, but he would bet money that it had been his great-granddad. *And there was no one there to help her. And look what came out of it.* More people suffered than anyone probably knew.

"I'll talk to her to see what exactly he'd done. If it is more than trying to snag a kiss or two, then I agree and she needs to speak up."

With that out of the way, Dylan decided to tackle the next subject, them. "You had asked to see me tonight. I assume it had nothing to do with Charlene."

"No. But I'm not sure you want to hear this. Not while driving."

He laughed. "You can't say that and then say nothing. Of course I want to know. How bad can it be?"

"Oh. It's about my mother. She thinks we're in love and she's going to talk to my father, who, in turn, will probably want to sit down and talk to you about your intentions."

That sure as hell wasn't anything he expected to hear. Dylan didn't even know how to respond. "They believe this why?" It had to be something Sofia told them, because he hadn't done anything to give such an impression.

"A customer said I had the look of someone in love in my eyes. My mother overheard the comment and it all went downhill from there."

"And you didn't correct them," he stated.

"I tried. Mama wasn't listening. Not that she ever does. That's why I'm in this predicament already."

"You, me, we."

"We?" she asked.

"Since your father wants to talk to me, then yes, it's we." It was time to come clean and let them know this was all an act. But if they did, they would never trust Sofia again. It would become a wedge in the family. "When is this talk supposed to take place?"

"I'm not sure. Mama didn't say. She said she was going to talk to my father. Oh, and my brother too."

"Have I told you I work best under pressure?" Dylan said. She shook her head. "So they believe we are crazy in love. I say we give them all the reasons why we want to take it slow, then show them how it *won't* work between us. If anything, I'm great at making parents not like me."

Sofia chuckled. "I have a hard time believing that."

"I wasn't always this charming, you know," Dylan joked.

"Really? You're charming?" Sofia teased right back.

"Exactly. Now what should be my not-so-charming traits

that you can't stand? And remember, they can't be so bad that my reputation will be ruined publicly, either."

"So saying I caught you trying on my underwear would be too much?"

Dylan burst out laughing. "Yes. How about you let me think of what it will be? You can just follow my lead." He shook his head and added, "I can just imagine what my brothers would've said once Sal shared that tidbit."

"Oh yeah, I forgot about that. But you're asking me to trust you on how to handle my parents. You would think I should be the one telling you."

"Since you can't even admit that you're in a play, I don't think you've got them wrapped around your pinky."

"And you do?" she asked.

"I don't know. How happy was your mother again to hear we are in *love?*" Sofia huffed and he added, "Told you, I'm charming."

"At least my mother thinks so," Sofia said.

And you know you do too. "I think we should take the proactive approach and set up the meeting. Why don't you tell them we're coming to dinner at the restaurant tomorrow night?"

"You're crazy, you know? My mother isn't someone you can mess with. She's able to see through bullshit like no one I know," Sofia said.

"Yet she thinks we're falling in love," Dylan said.

"Good point. Maybe she's slipping. Okay, I'll tell them in the morning when I go into work."

"I can't believe you work seven days a week. Why do you do it?" Of course, he was a workaholic himself.

"I guess I just fell into it. You'd never know it, but I have my college degree in business management."

"And you're waiting tables?" Why wouldn't they utilize her skills?

"Mama will never let go of the reigns. Even if she did, I'm not sure I want them. They have dedicated their entire lives to that restaurant. I can't remember them ever taking a vacation. I don't want that when I have a family. I want...I'm not sure what I want, really, but it's not that."

"Maybe we can use that as what breaks us up. I'm not willing to give up the city and you're not giving up the restaurant."

"I don't see how that helps me. I'll be stuck there for life after that," she said in a defeated tone.

"Or they'll see that they are holding you back and cut you free," Dylan stated.

He could tell she liked that plan, as her grin practically lit up the car. "You know Dylan, you might just be a genius."

I hope you remember that if it backfires. That only got her out of the restaurant, not out of the so-called relationship with him. *One thing at a time.* He just hoped no one found out that it wasn't real, or they'd both have some answering to do. Dylan had no plans of sharing their little charade. Actually, he had every intention of enjoying it as long as it lasted.

A distraction, but a sweet one, at least.

There was one thing this little road trip confirmed for him. Sofia was far more complex than one would think. She might be one of the sweetest women he'd met in a long time, but she was very unpredictable as well. He found the combination very...appealing.

Maybe my type has changed, and she's it.

9

Sofia really should've slept on the ride to Hudson, because there was no sleeping happening on the way back. Charlene was a chatterbox, which wasn't anything new, but this time she wanted to talk about anything but herself. That was different. Sofia knew she'd need to keep a close eye on Charlene over the next few days to make sure she snapped back to normal. Although she said nothing more had transpired, Sofia wasn't so sure. Then again, it could be that Charlene was just angry at herself for getting into that situation.

"Are you sure you're going to be okay?" Sofia asked on the staircase between floors.

"Yes, I am fine. I just want to go and soak in a hot tub and go to bed." Charlene turned to Dylan and added, "I'm warning you; you'd better not turn out to be an asshole too, or you'll have to deal with me."

Dylan said, "I'll keep that in mind."

Sofia gave Charlene a quick hug and watched as she headed up the final flight alone. When she was out of earshot, she turned to Dylan and said, "I hope she's going to be okay."

"I'm not an expert, but I think she will. She's tough."

"A lot tougher than I am, that's for sure. It's late, or maybe it's really early, but either way, did you want to come in and I can make you some coffee? I don't want to worry about you driving home alone and falling asleep at the wheel."

"Coffee sounds good. But you're tired and have to work in a few hours."

Her shoulders slumped. "Don't remind me. At this point I'm not going to bed. If I do, it'll be worse. So you might as well come in and have a cup. Consider it keeping me company for a while, not that seven hours in a car wasn't enough." She opened her door and said, "I can't believe you're not hightailing it out of here."

Dylan entered and closed the door behind him. "Charlene isn't the only one who was stressed by that incident."

Sofia nodded. "I guess so. No matter how much I told myself not to think the worst, I did."

"She's your friend. It's natural to care. Hell, I don't even know her and I felt for her situation."

And that just makes me like you even more. Sofia turned away and started scooping out coffee from the container and putting it in the filter. "You're not at all like I thought you'd be," she said.

"And is that a good thing?" Dylan asked.

"Yes."

"What did you expect?" he asked.

Sofia shrugged. "I'm not sure. Maybe someone arrogant. Kind of an ass. Not so caring."

"That sounds like me. Maybe you just don't want to see it."

She poured water into the back and pushed the button. "Maybe. Or maybe you don't want people to see the more sensitive side of you. I bet you watch Hallmark movies."

Dylan laughed so hard it echoed through her apartment. "You'd better hurry up with that coffee, because you're delusional now."

Sofia turned around and put her hands on her hips. "I'm not joking. You're not as tough as you pretend to be."

Dylan stepped closer so they were only inches apart. "Sofia, you're playing a dangerous game."

She looked up into his dark eyes. They were filled with frustration, exhaustion and maybe…desire. "I'm not playing Dylan. You're…different than anyone I've dated."

"I'm sure I am. But there is a lot you don't know about me, Sofia. Things you don't want to, either."

She eyed him and almost said they have a few hours before she had to be at work, but he was right, there was plenty she didn't know. The same went for him. Sofia had opened up to him more than she had many people. Actually, only Charlene knew her little secrets. *Probably better that way, too.*

"Okay, we'll save our…imperfections for when it's time to have my parents believe we can't stand each other."

Dylan laughed. "Maybe we can just make them up. They'd be a lot less…"

"Interesting?" she asked.

"Let's just say that being a Lawson comes with its good and bad things."

She reached out and took his hand, leading him to the couch. "Why don't you sit and tell me all about it?"

He stopped, and instead of sitting he said, "I'm not sure this is a good idea."

"What? You divulging all your secrets to me? I promise not to tell." *And I don't think you will be sharing anything anyway.*

Dylan shook his head. "I'm talking about me, you, us on the couch."

"I don't bite," Sofia stated.

"Biting doesn't worry me. It's everything that leads up to the biting that we probably don't want to act on."

"Are you talking about…"

"Sex," Dylan blurted out.

She would've used a different word, one not so bold, but he'd made his point. Sofia really hadn't been hitting on him. Flirting a bit. Okay, she wasn't opposed to having sex with him. Just look at him, he was gorgeous, and if he could make her feel as good in bed as he did just by talking to her, then it was going to be spectacular.

Don't even think about it. He said no. She totally got it too. Why add another complication to the ones they already had? And if the customers thought she wasn't concentrating on her job now, she could only imagine how bad it'd be after an all-nighter with Dylan.

Mama might just fire me. That actually was pretty tempting. It would resolve a few of her problems, of course, it would create another one. She wasn't making much money at all for doing the play. Really, it was enough to pay for parking, and only because she'd found an economy lot, and even that wasn't nearby. When she was lucky she caught the bus, and other times, she was forced to walk the rest of the way. Sofia hated to admit it, but she needed her job. And right now, she needed Dylan too, in more ways than she'd let him know.

"Dylan, why do men always think about sex? I wasn't even thinking about that." *Hardly. Well not much. Shit!* She would've ripped his shirt off and kissed him from head to toe, given the opportunity. Go figure it was Dylan who was bright enough to put it on ice.

Dylan still didn't sit. "I'm glad. Because we're having dinner at Mama's Place and I don't want you still flush."

She rolled her eyes. "A bit over-confident are you?" she asked.

"Not one bit. Now, if you don't mind, I'd better head back to the city. Are you sure you're going to be okay?" he asked.

No. I'm not going to do anything but think about you not being overconfident. "Of course I am. I'm going to study my lines before heading into work."

"What time should I pick you up?" he asked.

"Since I'm working there till one, why don't we just meet there and then you can offer to drive me home like a good *boyfriend.*"

He raised a brow and said, "I think you're enjoying this a bit too much."

Sofia waved her hand in front of herself and said in a southern drawl, "Who? Little ole me?"

Dylan laughed. "Goodnight Sofia. And I don't think you need to practice too much. Your acting skills seem spot on."

You mean the part about wanting you? Yup, all just an act. If she was going to study that scene with Dylan, it would be XXX-rated for sure. It'd been a while and her sexual frustration was peaking.

Not trusting her legs or any other part of her body right now, she said, "Thanks. Do you need me to walk you to the door?"

Dylan shook his head. "You sit and relax." He bent down and kissed her lightly on the lips before heading for the door.

Once she heard the clicking of the auto lock engaging, she let out a breath she'd been holding.

Sofia was glad he was gone. It was damn hard acting all the time. But she might as well put this time to good use. She reached for the script that was sitting on her coffee table. Sofia flipped it to page one and then closed it immediately.

"Is he freaking trying to kill me? I'm dying over here." It was a sweet torture, but still painful. Her body wanted what he obviously wasn't willing to give. Even her nipples ached. Tossing the papers back on the table, she got up and headed for her bedroom.

It wasn't going to be the same, but at least she had something hot to think about. *Sometimes you've got to take care of things yourself.*

When Dylan got outside, he found a police car parked directly behind him. He wasn't illegally parked, not that he really cared. He'd just pay the ticket. But he was concerned that it might have to do with Charlene. Maybe she'd changed her mind. If so, Sofia might want, or better yet, need, Dylan around a bit longer.

Although his reason for leaving was still hard in his jeans, it wasn't going to prevent him from being there for her. Walking over to the patrol car, Dylan stood by the driver's window. He rolled it down and instantly he recognized him.

"Sal, I didn't know you worked this shift."

"I don't. They were shorthanded so I offered. If I hadn't, I might not be here to see you leaving my sister's house at," he looked at his watch, "two o'clock. You do know she has to be at work in a few hours?"

She's a big girl and doesn't have a bedtime. Dylan also knew this had nothing to do with work, either. Dylan didn't have any sisters, and he never gave a shit what hour of the morning his brothers got in. Actually, he usually was the last one, if he came home at all. Those were the days, when he'd run all night and then sleep it off till noon the next day. Now he's up most nights working and hitting the gym before dawn. *Damn, I thought the twenties were supposed to be your wild years. I must have quit early.*

From the expression on Sal's face, he wasn't amused to be there. Dylan eased his mind. "She was just about to go to bed."

"And that is a good thing?" he asked.

"Since she's going *alone,* I thought you'd be happy," Dylan stated.

Sal glared at him. "Don't tempt me to haul your ass in, Lawson."

"For what? Keeping your sister out past her curfew? I'd like to see that on the report. Or maybe you'd rather I go back upstairs and knock on the door. I'm sure she's still awake."

"And I'm sure you're pushing your fucking luck. This is my sister you're talking about," Sal warned.

"I know. But she's also a grown woman who can make her own decisions. If she wants to be with me, I don't think there is anything you could do to stop her."

"You're one cocky bastard, aren't you? Charlie told me about you. Your youthful years were…questionable. I haven't asked him about who you are today, but there is something about you that says you haven't changed much. Maybe you just hide it better."

That was pretty accurate. Dylan replied, "Your mother likes me and more importantly, Sofia does. What you think really doesn't matter one bit." It was a hell of a lot of trouble to be going through for something that wasn't even true. Hell, he hadn't even had sex with her and Sal was riding his ass. This family really was overprotective. Then again, Sofia was worth protecting. She was unique, in more ways than he could count.

"Sal, I'd like to stand here and argue with you, but I have things that I need to do."

"At this time of night?" Sal snarled. "Nothing good happens at this hour."

Dylan laughed. "Then I really feel bad for you, because I can think of several things I enjoy all night. But then again, it's not a topic for the two of us." As Dylan turned to walk back towards his car, he added, "Have a safe night." He meant it. Dylan might be an asshole in several ways, but he respected the law and those who enforced it. It just wasn't a job for him. Hell, he'd spent a few years walking the fine line between legal and not.

Sal pulled his patrol car up to Dylan and said, "I'll see you at Mama's Place tonight. I think it's a *family* dinner." He was laughing as he pulled away.

I know. We set it up. It was good to know that Sofia wasn't the only one with acting skills. Sal didn't suspect anything, but Maria was another story. She could've worked for the CIA as an interrogator. If they could pull off dinner and make everyone believe he and Sofia are crazy about each other, then she would be free and clear to pursue her acting career. Because they'll all believe she was in the city with him.

This was good news for Sofia. For him, he was beginning to question what the hell his motivation was. At first, he told himself he was helping Sal's sister. But during their most recent talk, he'd been screwing with Sal. Was it smart pushing the guy's buttons when he'd been sitting in his uniform? No. Had it been fun? Unfortunately, yes. It reminded him of the old days when he did such things to his brothers. Either way, it helped blow off the frustration that had been built up within him. Not that he wanted to forget the taste of Sofia's lips, or the sexy curve of her body, but he didn't sit on that couch for a reason.

He'd left a long list of heartbroken women in the past. She wasn't going to be on it. Not if he could help it. *She is worth protecting, maybe even from me.*

Her heart was racing. Her shift was over and Dylan hadn't arrived yet. Of course, he was about to walk into the fire, or firing squad, by the look on Sal's face. She was surprised by his demeanor. Sal was the one she'd thought she *didn't* need to worry about. If she was wrong about this, what else had she missed?

Filippo came out of the kitchen and asked, "Is everything okay? You look worried."

"Papa, Dylan isn't here yet." That might be a good thing too. He could stand her up for their dinner date and she'd pretend to be crushed. Shed some crocodile tears and bam, it's over. *Why hadn't I thought about this before?* Maybe Dylan not showing was part of the plan, the part he'd forgotten to tell her about. But a good one, nonetheless.

"He will be here. He comes from the city and there's traffic to consider. If you're worried, maybe you should call him."

Should she lay out the groundwork and set the stage? It'd only been ten minutes. If he showed after, it'd be hard to backpedal. She'd give him a few more minutes, but if he didn't arrive soon, she was going to turn on the waterworks.

That was going to be difficult, because she wasn't a crier. It was something she feared having to do during a performance too. They said to dig deep into a part of her life, a memory or something that hurt so much, and think about that. Sofia was blessed, as she didn't have any of those experiences to draw upon—a problem many people wished they had.

"You're right Papa, I'm sure it's traffic." She went over and sat at the table with Sal. Might as well figure out what was bothering him before Dylan arrived. He looked exhausted. "Pulling double shifts again?"

He nodded. "Haven't slept yet so be wary, I'm short-tempered today."

"Today?" she teased. That familiar warning glare appeared immediately. Sofia couldn't help it. What were big brothers for, if not to push their buttons every once in a while?

"I can see one thing you and your *boyfriend* have in common."

Sofia could tell Sal didn't like calling Dylan that. "What is that?" she asked.

"You both like to prod the lion. Not wise, my dear sister. Not today. Unless you want me to spew what I've been biting back."

She wasn't sure what that meant. But since he'd included Dylan in that statement, it had to be about him. Sal wouldn't have used his police authority to do a background check on Dylan, would he? *Of course he would. He's overprotective.* The only question was, would he be revealing what he knows at dinner or privately? Sal had never thrown her under the bus before, and he had plenty of opportunities when she was growing up. Him being ten years her senior, he sometimes acted more like a father, than a brother. She wasn't sure which he was today. Whichever it was, he wasn't happy about her and Dylan.

"Sal, why don't you go home and get some rest? We can catch up tomorrow," she suggested. It wouldn't hurt not having him here, either.

Sal cocked a brow. "Trying to get rid of me?"

"Concerned for you. You look exhausted Sal. We're having a quick bite with Mama and Papa, then I'm going straight to bed myself." She wasn't sure how she'd even make it through dinner, her eyes burned so badly.

"You seem just as…tired. Maybe we both should blow off dinner. Why don't you let me give you a lift home?"

"Sal, you know I can't do that. I'm waiting for—"

"Your *boyfriend?* He doesn't seem to be coming."

This was really getting annoying, but so was sitting here and no Dylan. Sofia was just about to accept Sal's offer when she felt a hand on her shoulder and a kiss on her head.

"Sorry I'm late. I was with Charles. That niece gets cuter every day." He turned to Sal and added, "Charles said he got your message and will call you later, when the baby is asleep."

Sofia caught the twitch on Sal's jaw. Whatever he wanted to talk to Charlie about was supposed to be private. *Don't go looking for trouble when there isn't any.* After all, this wasn't real. It just felt that way.

"I'll call him after dinner. Which hopefully isn't cold now," Sal said.

Be nice. "Mama has never served a cold meal in her life. If you'll excuse me, I'm going to go let her know you're here and see if I can help bring things out." When she got up, she realized that would be leaving Dylan alone with Sal. That was a horrible idea. "Dylan, would you mind giving me a hand?"

"I'd love to." As they walked towards the kitchen, he whispered, "Everything okay with you two?"

So Dylan picked up on it, which meant her parents surely would too. "Yes. He's just working too much. Gets to us all."

"You must be talking about your brother," Mama said when they entered.

"Yes, Mama. He's so tired."

"You look the same, my dear." Then Mama looked around at Dylan and said, "You as well." With a loud belly laugh, she said, "Papa, look. These youngsters can't keep up with us."

Papa finished plating the food and peered around her mother. "That's because we have each other to lean on."

Maria smiled. "Such a romantic." Then she turned to Dylan and asked, "Are you?"

Dylan asked, "Romantic?"

She shook her head. "Someone to lean on? My daughter, can she count on you to be there if things are difficult, if she's tired, or sick? Will you care for her at all times?"

Dylan opened his mouth, but Sofia saved him. Quickly reaching for a plate, she purposely toppled it over onto the floor. "Oh no. I'm sorry. Let me clean it up." She dropped down to her knees but tilted her head and gave Dylan a wink.

"I'll help you," Dylan said.

"Oh, Papa, look at them. They are working together, just like us," Maria said, holding her apron up to her eyes, as though the sight brought tears.

Papa said, "All of you, out of my kitchen. I will make another and we will all eat in a few minutes. Now go before anyone spills anything else."

Dylan rose and offered Sofia a hand up as well. "Thank

you Papa." She kissed him on the cheek before she and Dylan headed back to their table.

Once out of earshot, he whispered in her ear, "Nice save."

"Can't promise it won't be brought up over dinner, but for now, you're in the clear." With any luck, their brief display was enough to appease her parents. Sal, on the other hand, was going to be harder to sway. As they sat down, she noticed Sal glaring at Dylan. In just a few minutes, her parents would join them. It had to come out now. "Sal, what is wrong with you tonight?"

"Ask Dylan," he replied.

She didn't. "This is between you and me."

Sal turned to her and said, "I think you're moving too fast. You've only known him for a little over a week and you're already sle—"

"Salvatore. Don't you dare say it. What Dylan and I do or don't is absolutely none of your business," she snapped. "And what makes you think we are?"

"He was there pretty late last night," Sal stated.

"You're spying on me?" Her mouth gaped in shock.

"No. I was working and happened to drive by and saw his car."

"Same thing Sal, and you know it," she snarled. "You wouldn't want me intruding in your personal life like that, so please don't do it in mine."

"So you're denying anything serious happened?" Sal asked.

Dylan chimed in. "I believe she's answered that."

"And you're what now? Her protector? How are you going to be that when you live in the city and she lives here?" Sal asked.

"Easy. She can move in with me," Dylan said.

Sal's eyes went dark and his fist clenched but nothing

topped the shriek from her mother behind them. Sofia could hear but not understand what she was sputtering under her breath in Italian. But it wasn't good.

Slowly she turned to see both her parents standing there holding trays of food for them to eat. Right now, she wasn't sure Dylan wasn't about to wear it. Sofia got up and said, "Mama, you should've called and I would've come help." Taking the first tray from her mother, she placed it on the stand. Then she did the same for her father.

Maria, still muttering, walked over close to Dylan. He didn't say a word, he didn't even flinch. If he was scared, he didn't show it. *You should be.* It was her father who spoke up in English first.

"Dylan, I do hope that we walked into a conversation that was about the future and not now," he said firmly.

Sofia jumped in. "Papa, he was just talking about protecting me."

Her father looked down at her. "From who? Are you in danger and we don't know about it?"

"No Papa. In general. You know how men talk. Sal was just voicing his concerns and Dylan just—"

"Asked you to live with him," Maria spoke up. "I think this dinner is overdue."

"No, Mama. He was just making conversation." Sofia wasn't sure what the hell Dylan had been doing when he suggested such a thing. Boy, he had them all riled up now.

Her parents sat down and looked directly into Dylan's eyes. "You are Charlie's brother, so we're accepting you. But if you hurt our daughter, you won't have any place to hide. Not even your money will protect you," her mother stated.

Papa patted her hand and said, "Mama, boys talk out of line sometimes. You should know how often Salvatore and Charlie did the same. And look, they are fine men now. I'm

131

sure Dylan wouldn't dream of taking your daughter from you and bringing her to the city. Isn't that right?" He turned to Dylan.

Please agree. She pleaded with him through her eyes. Dylan said, "Sofia is a very special woman and I'd never do anything to hurt her." He never took his eyes off her as he spoke, and it sent chills down her spine.

That wasn't an answer, but it also showed her parents that he wasn't one who'd back down. He'd fight for her. *Or at least he's great at pretending to.*

"Well that's settled, so can we eat now before it gets cold?" Sal said to break the tension.

She knew it wasn't over between the two men, but even Sal didn't want his parents in the middle of it. Not yet, at least. But she was sure, Sal and Dylan were going to finish this conversation later. *Hopefully not today.* They were all too tired, and their fuses were short. The last thing she wanted was for this to end in physical blows. From the looks in their eyes, her fear was justified.

Thankfully, things seemed to quiet down after that. There was a lot of talking, but it was much more casual. That all had to do with Dylan. Somehow he'd been able to get them to talk more about Charlie than him. Sofia once again had been left impressed by his skills. This time it was managing a room, even one made up of strong personalities like her mother.

Now if only he could just as smoothly convince everyone they weren't a couple, that would be great. Because by the time their little dinner was over, her parents were more convinced they were in love than before. All she had wanted was to be in a play, and now acting seemed to be all she was doing. Sofia knew somehow this was all going to bite her in the ass someday. *And damn it, I'm not sure how I'm going to explain it, either.*

. . .

Dylan knew he needed to maintain control of the conversation during dinner. There was one thing they were all waiting to hear: that he was in love with Sofia. Those were words he'd never spoken to a woman, and he sure as hell wasn't about to do so because her family wanted it. They had no idea; he wasn't the catch they thought he was. Well, Sal already might have come to that conclusion on his own.

Even Sofia didn't seem like herself after dinner. The ride to her house wasn't long by any means, walking distance on a nice day. Yet, the silence in the car made it seem long. He needed to find out what was bothering her, but his gut said it was him. He'd done his best not to fuck it up tonight, but right from the start, it was downhill. He wasn't sure how he was going to fix it, but he had to try.

"Sofia, I'm sorry I was late," he said.

She didn't even look at him as she said, "That was the least of the issues." Her voice was filled with frustration.

"Should I go through the list of things I'm sorry for, or can I just cover it in one shot? I know this was not how you saw tonight going."

Sofia turned to him and snapped, "You implied that we were having sex to my brother."

"No. I said that I could protect you. At no time did I mention sex," he defended. Dylan didn't want to think of his actions as being that crass, though they had been.

"What do you think Sal thought when you said you'd have me live with you? And worse than that, my parents heard it. I can only imagine what it's going to be like tomorrow when I see them."

"I explained that it was hypothetical," Dylan stated.

He pulled up in front of her building and she got out of

the car. Before slamming the door, she said, "What's funny is you really think they bought that? Right now, my parents are probably home discussing our wedding thanks to you. I knew I shouldn't have gone along with this."

Dylan got out of the car and followed her inside. He wasn't going to let tonight end on this note. "Sofia, we're both tired and blowing this way out of proportion. You'll see. When you go into work tomorrow, the only thing they will think is that we really like each other a lot."

He saw her stomping up each stair. She didn't send him away, which was a good sign. But what did it matter if she did? They weren't really a couple having their first quarrel. Unfortunately, it felt like it.

As they made it to her door and she unlocked it, he added softly, "I'm sorry Sofia. Those words came out of my mouth, and I have no idea why. I've never asked a woman to live with me before. Hell, I've avoided such commitment. So if you think you were shocked, I surprised myself." That was the truth. He definitely hadn't planned on saying anything even close to what he had.

Sofia turned and looked at him, "Then why did you?"

Looking down at her, he answered as honestly as he could. "Living together? I don't know where that came from, but I meant what I said about protecting you, Sofia. I won't ever let anything happen to you."

"Dylan, this isn't a conversation for the hallway. Either come in, or we can talk about this another time."

He should leave. Dylan told his feet to turn and walk away. Instead, he walked through her open door and closed it behind him. "Are you making me coffee?"

"Is this conversation going to take that long?" she asked.

He shrugged. "It might help clear my head. Somehow

with you around, things aren't always so...clear." *And that's how I say shit I wish I hadn't.*

Sofia pursed her lips. "So you're blaming this on me? I don't think so. I knew exactly what the plan was. Well...kind of. You're the one who took the detour." She walked over to the kitchen and started the coffee. He followed and sat at the table as she continued. "Come to think of it, this entire thing was your idea. 'Let people think we're dating. It'll be a great cover story.' There's a big leap from dating to, 'She can live with me in the city.' A simple breakup, we don't see eye to eye, isn't going to fly anymore. My parents still think I'm a virgin, for goodness' sake." She turned and added, "Well, they did until dinner, thank you so much."

"You're serious, aren't you?"

"Of course. I've been very successful at keeping my personal life separate from family. Thankfully I have Charlene upstairs, who would cover for me."

"But you're an adult. It's nobody's business what you do."

Sofia laughed. "I'm not sure what your family life is, if you guys are close or anything, but that's not how the Marcianos function."

"My brothers say shit, they always have an opinion. I just don't give a fuck. I'm almost twenty-nine, not twelve. Hell, when I was twelve, I didn't listen."

She put her hands on her hips and said, "And look at you now."

"Successful. Independent. A go-getter."

"Arrogant. Stubborn. And—"

"I get it. I should've listened. But all these things are what make me good in business," Dylan stated.

"But they don't work with women. Not in a relationship." Sofia blushed. "I'm not saying we have one. I know, this is all just an act. But if it weren't, you couldn't be all those things. A woman wants to be listened to, heard, and... taken seriously, not blindsided, like you did to me at dinner."

He'd hurt her and she just wasn't telling him. How dumb could he be? This little plan of his hadn't been thought through at all. Like his comment to Sal, it had been blurted out. Dylan wasn't used to doing that. It was out of character for him. Sofia might not like the fact that he blamed her, but this was *all* about her. She was the common denominator. She was the one fucking with his mind.

"You're right. I need to learn to do things...differently. But let me clarify something. This isn't a game. I like you. I meant what I said. I won't let anything happen to you."

She stared at him and asked, "Are you saying that..."

"I meant everything at dinner tonight. You are special Sofia, and don't forget it. And when I'm an asshole, like tonight, feel free to put me in my place. Hell, tell me to take a fucking walk, if you need to. Don't let anyone, even me, tell you what to do."

That was probably the most serious talk he'd ever had with a woman, but hopefully it clarified where they stood. She didn't say anything and just stared. When she did speak, she was back to her normal self.

"So, let me get this straight, when you said you wanted coffee, I could've said, 'You know where the pot is'?" she teased.

Dylan nodded. "And then you would've tasted the worst coffee of your life. But yes, that's what I mean."

Sofia's body language relaxed and she turned back to the dark brew. "I think I'm going to like this new arrangement."

"I'm glad." He wanted her to feel comfortable with him. Trust him.

"So, since this seems to be fifty-fifty, then I have a favor to ask."

"Anything," he said. Dylan usually wanted the details first before agreeing, but she wasn't one who would take advantage. She turned back with a wicked grin plastered on her face. He couldn't imagine what she was going to ask for.

"Tomorrow is the first rehearsal and I'm not ready at all. How do you feel about doing a read-through on the lines while we have coffee?"

Dylan raised a brow and said, "I'm not sure I'm the one you want helping you."

"Oh I am. I've witnessed your acting skills firsthand. And actually, at this point, I'm thinking you could be my acting coach."

She appeared to be serious, which was comical. "Hate to break it to you, but the only live theater I attended was forced upon me when I was young. I'll be happy to listen to you run through your lines, because it's you. Other than that, count me out."

"You never know. Maybe your taste has changed and you might enjoy it now," Sofia coaxed.

"I hated string beans when I was a kid and I still do today. I don't have to try something a second time. Like you said, I'm stubborn," he replied. Dylan might enjoy being with her, but he wasn't going to change for anyone, not even her.

"Or you just pretend to be stubborn," Sofia said with a wink as she handed him his mug. "Now you stay right there while I get the script." He heard her mutter, "This is going to be so much fun."

It was a good thing she'd made that coffee, because he was running on fumes. Two nights and maybe a total of six hours sleep. If he didn't stop, he was going to crash and it'd start affecting his work. Sofia wasn't in any different shape.

Although she looked beautiful as always, he hadn't missed the puffy eyes. If him staying and doing this with her would help, then damn it, he'd do it. *Even if it sucks.*

When she returned, she asked, "Are you ready?"

"I am, but you look like you could use some sleep."

"Exhaustion hit me about six hours ago. Now I'm so tired I barely know my name," Sofia said as she collapsed on the couch.

Dylan walked over and sat beside her. "Can I make a suggestion?"

"Don't you dare say I don't need to study, because I do," she said firmly.

"That's not what I was going to say. Why don't you sleep now and come into the city early tomorrow? I can run through these lines with you then, and it'll still be fresh in your mind for the rehearsal." He was working at Grayson Corp., and could use the distraction then.

"Dylan, I don't want to disturb you at work."

"Actually, the only thing I have going on is a meeting with Patty from A Fresh Day. She's coming to give me all the details regarding their services and financials."

Sofia's eyes widened. "You're going to sponsor them?"

"I'm meeting to gather more information. Sponsorship isn't something we take lightly." They were big on giving back, but there were people out there who only helped themselves, and the Lawsons distanced themselves from those so-called charities.

"We can study this tomorrow if you let me sit in on the meeting," Sofia said.

Dylan cocked a brow, totally puzzled. At no point did she strike him as the office type. "Sofia, the meeting might be long and boring." *Most are.* "I'm sure you have much better things to do than sit through it."

"I'd love to learn more about the agency. Actually, if I had any time to spare, I'd like to go back and volunteer."

He shook his head. "If you don't find a way to balance things in your life, you're going to burn out and possibly make yourself sick. There'll be time for working with these types of charities, but right now, isn't it. Not for you, at least."

"Are you telling me no?" Sofia asked with her arms crossed.

"I wouldn't dare. I was only advising. Do as you wish, but I learned a few years ago, if you try to take on the world, you spend more time spinning your tires in the sand and don't get far."

"You mean with Lawson Steel?" she asked.

"No. I wanted to be bigger, greater, and have my own company. All while working at Lawson Steel and trying to have a very active social life too. What ended up happening was, my father almost fired me, I had a reputation for reckless behavior, and my dream company, well, let's just say I don't have it."

Sofia sat back and said, "That's what I fear. I'll go for the gold and end up with nothing."

"You can go for it, but you need to make a better plan. All this running back and forth to the city is time you could be spending on your dream."

"Yeah, but it's too expensive to live in the city, and then I'd be running back to the restaurant. What difference would it make? None," she said, sounding defeated.

"Unless you take a break from the restaurant for a while."

She laughed. "And do what? I still need to support myself."

Sofia was right. And if he offered her a handout, she wouldn't take it. No different than that five hundred dollars he'd given her when they'd first crossed paths. She needed a job. One in the city.

"What are you good at besides being a waitress?" Dylan asked. He was about to ask if she was good with kids. Maybe Rosslyn could use help with childcare. But once again, this dark-haired beauty blew him away.

"I have my bachelor's in business management. I guess I could apply at some stores there, to manage them."

"You're serious aren't you?" Dylan asked.

"Why would someone lie about that?" she asked.

Dylan laughed. "If you'd ever worked in human resources, you'd see many do. But this changes everything. Do you think you can get some time off from the restaurant?"

"I'm sure I could…if I had a reason to, that is."

"Good. Is it too late to call your parents now?"

Sofia nodded. "Why?"

"Because I have a business proposition for you. One I think you'll like." He didn't have time to do all the research needed on A Fresh Day and then get another presentation prepared for Rosslyn. But why couldn't he hire Sofia to do it for him?

"I'm not working for you Dylan. That would make things…complicated."

She was right, it would. "I was thinking about Grayson Corp."

"You can't offer me a job for a company that isn't yours, either. I'm tired, but not asleep," she said sarcastically.

"I'm filling in for Rosslyn while she's out on maternity leave. She owns Grayson Corp. So technically, I can hire you to work for her. And from what I see, she's missing a liaison, someone who has time to research and meet with agencies like A Fresh Day."

"I thought you were doing that tomorrow?" Sofia asked.

"I am, but that means I'm not working on contracts for Lawson Steel. I'm spreading myself out too thin again. And if you take on doing this, then I can do what I need to do." *And get you in the city.*

"That sounds great, but Dylan, you're forgetting one thing. I live here. I'd still be traveling every day. The only difference would be who I work for. I think I should just keep things as they are."

"Unless you stay with me," he said.

Her eyes darkened and she huffed. "Dylan Lawson, that's the second time today you've pulled that crap. Is this some kind of game you're playing to get me into your bed?"

In a serious tone, Dylan replied, "Sofia, if that were my goal, all I'd need to do is this." He leaned over and gently placed his lips on hers. A soft moan escaped her and she leaned into him. It'd be so easy to pull her onto his lap and continue. But she was exhausted and when he did have her, he wanted to make sure she was well rested. *Because you're going to need it.*

Pulling away, he looked down at her. She cleared her throat and blinked several times to open her eyes. "I guess… you…made your point." Sofia let her head rest on his shoulder. "And this is why I shouldn't live with you."

"Afraid we won't hold back?" he asked.

She shook her head. "Nope. I already know the answer." Snuggling closer she added so softly, it was barely a whisper, "We won't."

He could tell from her breathing that Sofia had fallen asleep. Dylan wasn't about to wake her. She needed rest most of all. Slipping out from beside her, he guided her down to lie on the couch. Then he slipped off her shoes and put her feet on the couch. There was a small blanket on the rocker and he covered her. Placing a kiss on her forehead, he said, "Sweet dreams," before letting himself out.

As he got into his car, he realized she hadn't answered him about the job or the living arrangement. It's funny that she said she didn't want anyone telling her what to do, when in reality, he didn't believe she'd ever allow it to happen in the first place. *I don't think I'm the only stubborn one.* It just looked better on her.

"You did what?" Gareth snapped. "Without speaking to Rosslyn or Charles? You've really lost your fucking mind."

"I really think I have," Dylan said. "All this shit with Granddad and the Hendersons and Aunt Audrey has my head spinning. That's got to be what is screwing with me. I've never asked anyone to live with me. *Never.*"

"Keep it up Dylan, and you're going to end up like Charles. Not that it's a bad idea. I mean, with you off the market, that just means more ladies for me," Gareth teased.

"That's a leap, living together and getting married. Besides, she didn't say yes."

"Wait, she turned you down? You failed to mention that. You're in trouble now."

"Gareth, it means she's not interested in that," Dylan added.

"You're right. It means she wants it all. You know, the house, white picket fence, ring on her finger, and five kids running around."

"Sofia never said she wanted those things," he stated.

"Did she say she didn't?" Gareth asked.

Fuck. No. This was the lecture he'd given Sofia yesterday. If you take on too much, things start to slip. With Dylan, it was how *not* to get snared. Was that what Sofia was doing, getting him to chase her? What did she have to gain? He wasn't about to marry her. He wasn't marrying anyone. The single life was perfect with him. Like Gareth said, there were plenty of women out there, all he had to do was pick up the phone and he had a date.

So what the hell was he doing right now? Sitting down with a family for dinner, one that wasn't his, definitely gave the impression this was heading in that direction. All of this was supposed to be an act. That kiss last night hadn't been part of any plan. Her response to him hadn't been fake, either. Actually, Dylan had asked her to live with him because he enjoyed her company that damn much and wasn't ready for it to end. She was a distraction, but one he found suited him, not that he'd admit that to anyone, even having a difficult time admitting it to himself.

Yet when she spoke about her future and what she wanted, it seemed like she'd only be in New York City during the run of the play. Once again, he'd found himself caught up in the moment with her and he hadn't asked her important questions, like how long would that be? One month? Two? Six? Gareth might be busting his balls, but shit, he'd called it. Dylan wasn't himself right now. Before he moved any further, he needed to figure out why. No woman had ever been so captivating that he lost control before, and surely she wasn't going to be the first. It had to be something else.

He ran through the list of things he liked about her. One was she wasn't pushing or demanding in any way. Actually, that seemed to be him. It fit his business motto, but not dating life. She also wasn't out chasing him. He'd forgotten what it was like to be with a woman who wasn't looking at him for

144

what she could get. The only chasing Sofia was doing was on her own dream.

Dylan knew he wasn't looking for anything serious, anything long-term. Sofia probably wasn't looking to get tied down either. The only way to confirm they were on the same page, was to ask the questions.

"She's coming to the city in a few hours, we can talk more about it then," Dylan said.

"And when are you going to let Rosslyn know about the wonderful job offer you put out there? Remember, she has enough to worry about without thinking you're going to make any drastic changes to her business plan."

"I guess I should stop over there when I leave here." Dylan wasn't worried about Rosslyn not approving; he was more concerned she'd love the idea and expect more like it. He was supposed to sit in her chair, not actually drive the business.

"Want company?" Gareth asked.

"No. The only reason why you're interested in joining me is in hopes that Charles flips out," Dylan stated.

"Damn. Maybe I should ask Sofia for some acting tips so you can't read me so well," he teased. "What time will she be here?"

"You really have too much time on your hands. Why don't you be useful and look into Tabiq for us?" He hadn't forgotten anything Brice had told them, and he wasn't about to let it drop either. "Brice said our great-granddad was involved. I want to know what that meant."

"Brice made it clear that we probably didn't want to know."

"I don't give a shit what Brice thinks. He's protecting his own interests. If I've learned anything from all this, it's that the person who knows the most, holds all the cards. Right now, I feel like that's Brice."

"He's not about to do anything with the information. I actually got the feeling he was hoping to mend the family someday," Gareth said.

Dylan leaned back in his chair and said, "How do you expect that to happen when the family isn't supposed to know that we're related?" Gareth didn't reply. "Exactly. And while you're digging into Tabiq, pull everything you can find on all the Hendersons. I never want to be blindsided again."

"Dylan, that would be like picking a fight. I can't stress how unwise that is. Hendersons might be blood relations, but they won't take being fucked with."

"So you just want to sit back and pretend we don't know there's more?" Dylan asked.

"I'm saying timing is everything. This is not it. Let Charles enjoy his new baby and when things settle down, we'll pull together as a family and discuss the next course of action. Until then, I think we have more to lose than to gain."

"That's not what you thought when you went after Maxwell Grayson," Dylan reminded him.

"That was different."

"How?"

"Maxwell intentionally fucked with Dad and tried to ruin Lawson Steel. The Hendersons are as much victims in all this shit as we are. And from the look in Brice's eyes, I'm not sure they didn't suffer more. At least Aunt Audrey wasn't around to torment us for long."

Dylan knew Gareth was speaking logically, but he needed something to focus on besides Sofia. She was beginning to fill his thoughts day and night. Something had to give to let out all this built-up frustration.

"I'll let it rest for now. But if I find out any of the Hendersons are digging into our lives again, the gloves come off."

"I'm with you on that," Gareth said. "But I don't see how putting this on hold for six months or so is going to change anything. And besides, we have other things we need to focus on. With Charles off playing daddy, and you playing….well let's just say I'm not sure what you're doing right now, but you're preoccupied too, but that means the weight of the workload is falling on us four. I even had to blow off a date last night to finish reviewing a contract that had to be signed today."

"Oh poor Gareth, a night home alone. Did you want me to call Dad and tell him you need his help after all?" Dylan said sarcastically.

"Fuck no! That's the last thing we need."

"I thought so. And by the way, I'm not *playing* around. I'm managing Grayson Corp, *and* still maintaining my job here at Lawson Steel. If something is falling behind, don't look at me." Dylan didn't give any or take any excuses for shit not getting completed on time. The success of Lawson Steel was first and foremost on his mind. *Most of the time.*

"You want to go grab lunch?"

"No. I'd better go see Rosslyn before she hears it from someone else," Dylan said, giving Gareth a warning look.

"Hey, I wouldn't tell her."

"No. You'd tell Seth, who'd tell Jordan, who'd tell Ethan, who would somehow let it slip. I know how this works. The only secrets are the ones you don't share."

"Hey, right now the only talk is about the baby, so talking about your love life is exactly what we need," Gareth said. "Well, go tell her you hired your *girlfriend*. I'll keep my ears open for the repercussions later."

Getting up to leave Gareth's office, he said, "You're a real ass sometimes."

Gareth laughed. "Wow, that's an improvement. I must be getting soft in my old age."

Dylan shook his head and left. There was no winning with Gareth today. And really, there was no point in arguing. Dylan wasn't retracting the offer. And that's how he was going to present it, too.

He spent the next two hours updating Rosslyn on everything he'd learned so far, and what he believed Grayson Corp. was missing.

"I totally agree with you, Dylan. My uncle wasn't a very...charitable person. The more he had, the more he wanted. I'd like you to dig deeper into A Fresh Day. There are several others that might need help as well. Charles let me know all the things Lawson Steel has been doing over the years. I don't want to duplicate their, your, efforts. I think bringing someone on full time who can be on the streets, talking to the people, will help me get a better understanding of where Grayson needs to be."

On the streets? That wasn't where he wanted Sofia to be. How would he protect her? Granted, she'd probably love the idea, but he wouldn't. "I was thinking more like an office job."

"Anyone could do that. Heck, I could have my assistant Liz do that instead of playing on social media. No, I want to get up close and personal with people, make sure we're not being sold on only what some agency wants us to know. All businesses, non-profit or not, have their own agenda."

That was true. And Rosslyn impressed him. Grayson Corp. was in good hands with her at the helm. Now how was he going to explain to Sofia that the job was no longer available? Because there was no way in hell he was allowing her to take it.

Dylan walked over and gave Penelope a kiss on the forehead before leaving. Things definitely weren't the same around here. Business meetings were being held with babies around. Decisions were changing as often as diapers. What the hell was next? Was this the new norm? If so, Dylan wasn't sure how he was going to adapt.

When he got outside, he took a few deep breaths and tried to prepare himself for the next half of the day. Unfortunately, what he thought would be easy, wasn't.

How do I keep getting myself into this shit? The answer was Sofia's honey-brown eyes. They were going to be the death of him. A slow, painfully sweet death — one he couldn't seem to walk away from, either.

Sofia took more notes than Dylan seemed to. Had he meant it when he said he wanted her to take the job, and this was day one? She hadn't accepted the job, then again, she hadn't declined it, either. Listening to Patty talk filled her with an excitement that she hadn't expected.

Maybe it wouldn't be so bad taking a break from Mama's Place to try something new. It'd give her a chance to use her degree, as well. It all sounded perfect, but she knew nothing was. Making this change would come with difficulties, if not for her, then for her parents. They counted on her, too much. That's why she was still there. Was it time to have the conversation about leaving? She'd tried it several times before, but they wouldn't sit long enough for her to make them listen. With Dylan in the picture, they might be expecting it. *They might be expecting me to say we're getting married, too.* Always a complication.

Sitting there tapping her notepad with her pen, Sofia looked up and noticed Dylan was staring at her. "What?"

"You seem…distracted," he said.

"I was thinking about the meeting. I thought it went well. But as you know, I've helped out there one day. It doesn't seem to be enough now. Not after learning all the details." She had told herself she'd go back. But lack of time was the only obstacle. She couldn't imagine how she'd be able to fix that. If anything, it was about to get worse since rehearsals start.

"I'm not talking about A Fresh Day. There seems to be more than that on your mind. Is everything okay with Charlene?" Dylan asked.

She smiled. It was nice that he didn't put business before all else. "Yes, she's better. We spoke on the phone during my drive here. She swears she'll never do anything that stupid again. I'm not so sure about that, but at least she knows she was lucky, and might not be next time."

"We all choose our own paths."

Sofia let out a sigh. "Or our parents choose them for us. I know what I want, I just need to do it."

"What do you want Sofia?"

She looked down at the notepad and knew this was now part of her plan — well, if you could call it that. The wants in her mind were jumbled up, and she needed to sort them out, prioritize them.

"It's easier to say what I don't. Now I just need to go home and tell my parents. Dylan, I'm not sure I would be able to do this if it weren't for you."

"Me? I have a feeling you can do anything you set your mind to."

"Thanks. I try, but my mother—"

"Loves you and wants you to be happy. That's what every

mother wants for their child. All you need to do, is show her what makes you happy."

Sofia laughed. "You make it seem so easy. Maybe you should go and talk to her for me," she teased.

He didn't even crack a smile. "Sofia, if I thought that was answer, I'd do it. If you need me there as support, that's fine. But in my opinion, you'll do better on your own."

"Now I just need to find the time to do it. I have to study, then I have rehearsal tonight. By the time I get home, it'll be too late."

"Can you read in a moving vehicle without getting sick?" Dylan asked.

"Don't know. Haven't tried it. Why?"

"If we leave right now, you have time to make it to Mama's Place, and back."

She put the notepad down on her lap and said, "You're serious, aren't you? You want me to do this right now."

"No. You want to do this; I'm only providing the means to make it happen. Do you want the ride or not? I'm not pushing you Sofia, this has to be your decision," Dylan said with his elbow resting on his desk. "I support you, whatever you choose to do."

That was so foreign to her. Everyone had a strong opinion, and if you didn't listen to them, you were wrong. She wished she had time to think more about this. Then again, she'd been thinking about it for years, she just hadn't done anything about it. Getting up, Sofia slammed the notepad on his desk and said firmly, "Let's get going. I'm ready."

Dylan eyed her for a second before rising himself. "Watch out world, here she comes."

Sofia wrinkled her nose and said, "It's not the world that scares me."

He walked around the desk and took her hand. "Don't worry, Mama loves me."

"Yeah, but I have a feeling Sal doesn't. Maybe you can enlighten me on what happened on the way to the restaurant."

"And maybe you should just study your lines. Don't worry about Sal. He's just a big brother watching out for his sister."

"But he likes the Lawson family," she added.

"That doesn't mean he wants any of us sleeping with you."

"But we're not." *Yet.*

"You'll never convince him of that. He knows our reputation. It hasn't always been good." Dylan turned to his assistant, Liz, and said, "Call my cell phone if there is anything urgent. Otherwise, I'm gone for the day."

"And if Rosslyn calls, what should I tell her?" Liz asked.

"The truth," Dylan said as they walked towards the elevator.

"And what is that?" Liz called out.

"I'm out with Sofia," he replied.

Sofia heard what sounded like giggling from Liz. "You're going to start rumors that we're involved."

Dylan raised their hands, which were still joined. "Do I look like I care?"

She smiled and said, "No. And for the first time, I don't either."

"Good. You keep that attitude for when you meet with your parents," he said.

That wasn't going to be possible. "You won't be holding my hand then."

He shook his head. "I've seen how driven you are. It's your time to make your move, go your own way. You don't need me."

No. But I want you. "You just made it all possible. Without your job offer and letting me stay at your place, I couldn't do it. I have no idea why you're so...good to me, but I really appreciate it." She felt the muscles in his arm tighten for a moment. Had he forgotten this was all his idea? Did he have second thoughts? "Nothing has changed, has it?" She needed to know before she delivered the news to her parents.

"Nope. The offer stands."

He never looked at her when he replied. She was about to press him further, but instead the elevator door opened and they got on, no longer alone. This wasn't the time. And if Dylan really didn't want her there, he'd tell her. Wouldn't he? *Guess I'm about to find out.*

The ride wasn't as productive as she'd hoped. Reading in a moving vehicle didn't seem to be an issue; concentrating on what she read was. Dylan was right, she wasn't a child and should present herself as a confident woman. It wasn't lack of confidence or ability that had stood in her way all these years. Family was everything to her. No matter how she delivered the news that she was leaving Mama's Place, it was going to hurt them. It was something she dreaded doing.

Dylan pulled the car up in front of the restaurant and shut off the engine. "Want me to come in or not?"

Sofia wanted to decline his offer, but said, "In, but let me do the talking, if that's okay." He agreed, and together they entered. Thankfully it was during the lull in business. Only one customer was seated at a table and another at the bar. Emily could handle everything while she spoke to her parents.

"Sofia, I thought you were gone for the day?" Emily said. "Do you guys want a table? There's plenty to pick from," she teased.

"Just popping in for a few minutes."

153

"Oh. And you look serious too. Are you two getting—"

"No. We're not. I think the man at the bar is waiting for his drink, Emily." Sofia walked right past her and into the kitchen. Sure enough, her parents were there sitting down, taking their break, having a late lunch together. "Hi Mama, Papa, can we come in?"

"Of course. What are you two doing here?" Filippo asked.

She walked over and stood by the table. Dylan was right behind her. Was he there to support her or block her escape? Trapped was exactly how she felt at the moment. But the only way to change it was to say it.

"I needed to talk to you about…my working here. I've been offered a job that I *really* want and one that would make me very happy."

Maria's face saddened and she turned towards Filippo. He patted her hand and then Maria turned back to Sofia. "Tell us about this *wonderful* job."

"Well, it really is. And I think you'd both approve of it, too. I'd be doing hands-on research, working as a liaison between people in need and the charity organizations that provide help. What I learn will directly affect how funds are distributed, in order to make the largest positive impact on the community." *And I finally get to put my education to use.*

"Well, that does sound like a good job. We brought you up to know how one can make a difference. I guess you're going to show us just what you can do now, aren't you?" Maria asked.

"Yes, Mama. I'm sorry. I know that you dreamed of me being here always at Mama's Place, but this is what makes me happy." It really was, too. She wasn't giving up on her dream to be an actress, but instead, diverting her energy in a way that made sense to her.

"All we want is for you to be happy," her father added.

"I am," she said. "And I'm sure you'll find someone qual-ified to take my place. There have been plenty of applicants over the years."

"No one could ever take your place, Sofia. You're part of this place, just like we are, and Salvatore. You don't have to work here to remain part of it. You are family, and this is a family business," Filippo said.

"Thank you, Papa." She turned to her mother, who was still very quiet. "Mama, don't be angry with me."

"I'm not. But you haven't told us everything. Where is this new job?"

Sofia sucked in her breath. She'd known her mother was going to ask eventually. "Grayson Corp."

"The city?" she exclaimed. "No. It's too far. Too danger-ous. No one there to take care of you if something happens. You can't go there alone."

"She won't be. She'll be with me," Dylan spoke up.

Her mother looked at him and said, "This was your idea? To take our little girl away from us and bring her to a place loaded with crime?"

"It's not like that. I've lived there all my life, and have never witnessed any. Like anyplace, you just use your head and avoid people who are out looking for trouble."

Her mother started ranting in Italian, and her father whis-pered to her, trying to calm her. Sofia added, "Mama, it's going to be okay. Dylan would never let anything happen to me."

"Ha. How can that be?"

"She'll live with me. And I live in a very secure place. I promise, nothing will happen to her."

Dylan had delivered the bomb that set off the water-works. Her mother was crying on her father's shoulder. Sofia's heart was breaking as well. She had dreaded this day, but whether it be now or in a year or two, the results would be the same.

In a soft voice, Sofia pleaded, "Mama, please try to be happy for me."

Her mother broke away from her father and wrapped her arms around Sofia. "Oh Sofia, I am happy for you. Just sad for me. I thought someday you would change your mind and learn to love the restaurant. But my dream was not yours. It never was. Just like it wasn't Salvatore's either."

"You raised us to be strong and believe in ourselves, that we could be anything we wanted. So in a way, Mama, you got what you wanted, just not everything," Sofia said, trying to cheer her mother up.

"Dear Sofia, I had everything I wanted when I had you and Salvatore. This is just a building where we kept it all together. You are right. You're brilliant and Grayson Corp. is lucky to have you." Maria turned and looked at Dylan. "But you. I am holding you to your promise that nothing will ever hurt my little girl. *Especially not you.*"

"You have my word," Dylan replied.

"Are you two staying for dinner so I can call Salvatore and you can tell him the news?" her father asked.

"Papa, I need to get back to the city. There are things that I need to get set before I start."

"Back? You mean you were already there?" her mother asked.

"Yes, Mama. You don't get a job without meeting with the company first. Dylan has been kind enough to drive me around so I'm not alone." *Why he volunteered for this is still beyond me.*

"But you'll be back right? You're not going for good, are you?" she asked.

"Of course I'll be back. Mama, the city really isn't that

far, it just seems like it. But you can see the lights from here."
*The ones that have been calling to me for years. And now I'm
going to be living there.* It felt surreal.

Her mother huffed and demanded, "Call me every day, or
I will come to the city and take you back home. Do you
hear me?"

Sofia smiled. "Yes, Mama. Every day. I promise. I love
you."

"I love you too, my dear Sofia. Now you go and you
make a difference in that city."

"Yes, Mama. I'll try."

When she and Dylan were back in his car and on their
way to her apartment, only then did it all start to hit her. She
really was doing this. Her dream was now within her grasp.
How could so much change in just a few weeks? She looked
over to the man sitting beside her. *And I think a lot more
changes will be coming, too.*

Sofia was happy. But were they moving too fast? Was this
joy she felt fleeting, and soon she'd be left with regret? She
really didn't know what tomorrow was going to bring, but
right now, it felt right. If it all fell apart, at least she had
Mama's Place to fall back on, and at least she would've tried
her best.

Sofia didn't want to talk about it. She'd blown that rehearsal. The director had corrected her more times than not. It wouldn't surprise her if they asked her not to return. It'd be her own fault, too. She'd been given plenty of time to study the lines, and each time something had come up. Some were legitimate excuses, others not.

"Still thinking about what happened with your parents?" Dylan asked.

It'd make sense if she were, but that was the one thing that wasn't stressing her right now. They really seemed okay with her decision. Then again, what choice did she have? It wasn't like Sofia had gone asking for their permission. *Just their blessing.*

"It's been a long day all the way around," Sofia replied, not ready to discuss how horrible things had gone for her yet. That last thing she needed was Dylan questioning her acting skills, anymore than she was already. *I know what I need to do, I just have to do it. Tomorrow is another day and I'll be prepared.* Even if it meant studying during her lunch break, she would. It wasn't just the director and the other actors that she let down, it was herself too.

"It'll be better when we get to the apartment."

"And unload. That's something to look forward to," she said with a chuckle.

"I'll have it brought in, but the unpacking is all you." Dylan paused, then added, "I have a confession to make."

"It's too late, if you're going to tell me you're married."

He laughed. "Guess this will be easier than I thought. I...I wasn't expecting any of this today. So when you get inside, you might find my apartment is lacking a few things."

"Like what?"

"Food," he stated. She choked out a chuckle and he added, "I don't spend much time there. Just to sleep, mostly."

"Do you have any issue with me doing some cooking? I'm kind of particular about what I eat. Maybe it's because my mother is such a good cook."

"Please tell me she passed that talent down to you," Dylan said.

"Of course. I practically grew up in that kitchen." She sighed. "It's going to be weird not going in there every day."

"Having second thoughts? I mean, if you are, I can drive you back home, if that's what you want."

"Trying to get rid of me already? We haven't even made it up to your apartment."

"Sofia, I'm serious. I want you to be happy."

She saw the look in his eyes. It wasn't one that questioned his decision, but was questioning hers. "Leaving wasn't a spur-of-the-moment decision. I've been wanting to do this for many years. And for the record, I didn't do this for you, either. This decision was made based on what works best for me. At least, for now."

"Ouch. That's a kick to my ego," Dylan teased.

"You know what I mean. But if your ego needs some stroking, then know that I wouldn't have agreed to live with anyone else."

Dylan smiled. "My ego is intact, but I'm glad to hear that anyway. And don't let this go to your head, but I wouldn't have extended the offer to anyone else, either."

Surely someone like Dylan Lawson had women banging down his door to move in. She could only imagine how many had spent the night here in his bed. That thought didn't appeal to her one bit. She wasn't the jealous type, and really there wasn't anything to be jealous of. He was still just being supportive of her...acting career? She was just telling herself that, so there was no chance of getting hurt. But no man would go to this length. He cared about her and she...was only there because she cared about him as well. Just neither was ready to admit it.

"All I know is, I can't wait to get upstairs and get into a hot shower."

"Then why are we sitting in the car?" he asked.

"Because it's your place, and besides, I don't even know which apartment is yours," she teased.

He pointed to the top of the building. "All the way up."

She stuck her head out the car window and looked up at the skyscraper. "You're joking, right? That's the penthouse."

"To me, it's a place I lay my head. Lawson Steel builds skyscrapers or major developments all over the world. I take it you didn't know."

She continued looking at the building and said, "Dylan, when you asked me to live with you, I thought...well...that you had an apartment. Not...this."

"Sofia, can you please stop looking at the building and look at me," Dylan said, taking her hand in his. When she did so, he said, "Sofia, do you know what I like about you?"

"I believe you said my eyes."

Dylan grinned. "They are beautiful and I could stare into them for hours. But this isn't just something physical. And I hope you know that."

"If I thought so, I wouldn't be here now. But what does any of that have to do with your living arrangements?"

"Absolutely nothing. They are just things, things that don't mean much to me. If you're uncomfortable staying here, then tomorrow we can look for a place that might suit us both better."

She was shocked. "Dylan, this is your home. Why would you leave it?"

"I told your parents that you'd be here with me and I'd protect you. I meant that, Sofia. Part of that is making sure you're happy. If this place makes you uncomfortable, then we find someplace else. That simple."

Simple for you. "Dylan, I'm sure your place will be fine. Like yourself, I'm going to be working so much, I'll hardly be there either."

As they made their way up to his place, she couldn't help but wonder why she was feeling this way. It was ridiculous that she was even having thoughts like this. What his place looked like really shouldn't matter. Heck, her dream was the rich and famous lifestyle, and here she was, about to live it. But this wasn't hers, it was his, and she didn't want to get used to it. Most actresses lived a hard life until they got their break, if it ever came at all. Staying in a penthouse apartment in New York City, even for a brief time, was more than most would ever see.

Maybe that's what was troubling her, that it was beginning to feel more like a fairytale. Dylan was no prince, and he admitted to it, and she wasn't some damsel in distress who needed rescuing, either. So what did that leave? A relationship of...convenience? That didn't seem Dylan's style, and sure as heck wasn't hers. But if you removed the kisses from the equation, her being here really could be just a case of one person helping out another, no strings attached.

She'd been looking for her freedom for so long, and she finally had it. The last thing she wanted was to be tied down to anything or anyone. The best thing she could do was keep this, whatever it was, platonic. It wasn't going to be that hard. Well, as long as they never kissed or touched or got too close to each other. Then it was all over. Not only couldn't she hold back, she didn't want to. The sexual attraction between them was powerful. And although she thought she could act pretty well, hiding it from him was impossible.

Oh hell, who am I kidding? I don't want the PG fairytale version. What fun would that be?

When the private elevator doors opened up and they stepped out into his apartment, Dylan said, "You're awful flush. Don't like elevators?"

She hadn't even paid attention. "Guess I'm just a bit nervous about the next step." *More like anticipating. Excited. Desiring. But we'll go with nervous.* It sounded less...bold.

"I guess that is a good question. We never discussed sleeping arrangements. I do have a spare bedroom that you're welcome to." Dylan stepped closer and tipped her chin up to meet his gaze. "Or you can share mine."

Her heart pounded so loudly it seemed to fill the room. This is what she wanted. Why wasn't she falling into his arms and going for it? *Because falling is what I'm afraid of.* She liked him more than she wanted to admit, and it was going to hurt like hell when it was time to say goodbye. For someone like Dylan, it wasn't *if* that would happen, it was when. Was it better to have loved and lost than never loved at all? Was the pain worth the pleasure? *Guess I'm going to find out.*

162

. . .

What the hell is wrong with me? Dylan knew he was moving too fast; he wanted to put it out there and let her decide. But fuck, it was killing him to be so close and not pull her into his arms and kiss every inch of her. Never before had he wanted anyone the way he did her. It wasn't all about making himself feel good, although he knew he would. He wanted to please her even more than himself. Whatever she wanted, he'd respect and honor.

But those big honey brown eyes of hers staring back at him were driving him nuts. He could tell she was debating what she wanted. All it would take was for his lips to touch hers and he knew he could sway her decision. But that would be an asshole move. Not that he wasn't one, but he didn't want to be with her like that. If she needed time, she'd have it. No matter how tight the bulge in his jeans became.

The attraction to her was getting stronger each time he saw her. Knowing that they were traveling to the city to stay together had only enhanced his desire. All he wanted was one more taste of those sweet lips. At every traffic light, he fought the urge to pull her into his arms. He didn't, because he wouldn't have been able to stop. Her white blouse had been professional in the office, but now it was pressed tightly against her breasts by the seatbelt, her taut nipples teasing him, as though begging for his attention. It was no wonder his cock was aching.

So when Sofia stepped a bit closer and asked, "Which bed is more comfortable?" Dylan had her answer.

Wrapping an arm around her waist, he pulled her up against him and said, "I really don't know. Maybe we should give them both a try and find out."

"It's always wise to do your research before making a

decision. And I believe in being thorough, too," she said with a wink.

What little restraint he had was gone. "Holy shit woman, you're making holding back, very difficult."

"I'm sorry."

No you're not. He could hear the desire in her voice. It matched his own. Dylan gently touched her chin, tipping her face to look up at him. Her honey-brown eyes were now dark, her olive skin, flush. "Do you know how beautiful you are?"

"Tell me," she said seductively.

She laid a soft hand on his chest, instantly causing blood to rush through his veins. When she ran her hand lower, his muscles tightened. He moaned, gripping her more tightly, leaving little question about how much he wanted her.

"I'd rather show you," he said, his voice almost a growl. "I'm going to kiss you, Sofia. If you are not positive this is what you want, I suggest you tell me now. Because once I taste those sweet lips of yours, I'm going to want to taste *all* of you."

She opened her mouth, and he feared she was about to tell him no. If she did, he'd stop. He might need to put some ice in his pants to cool his jets, because even a cold shower wasn't going to be enough to put out this fire. But shit, he'd respect her wishes if no was her answer.

He felt her legs tremble against his and she reached up, wrapping her arms around his neck. That was all the invitation he needed. He bent to kiss her, slowly at first, tracing her lips with his tongue, teasing and encouraging her lips to open for him, which they did. He loved how she clung to his shoulders, pulling him even closer, wanting more. She was driving him over the edge, and this was only the beginning.

His hands found their way under her blouse to cup her breasts. Sofia moaned and arched her back. Dylan pulled them back out and his fingers struggled with each button, trying to be delicate, when all he wanted was to rip the fucking thing off. She must have picked up on his frustration and her hands replaced his. Finally, she slipped out of her blouse. Then she reached around and unhooked her bra, letting it drop to the floor and exposing her breasts.

Perfect.

His mouth was back on her, this time trailing kisses slowly down her neck, to her collarbone, and finally stopping at her breast. Taking one nipple gently to his mouth, he sucked and nibbled it until her moans filled the room. Then he moved his attention to her other breast, repeating the process. Her hands ran through his hair, and she seemed to be prodding him lower.

"Don't worry sweetheart, I'll get there," he nipped her nipple, "eventually."

"Dylan, please," she pleaded.

There would be plenty of time for slow, but he didn't want to rush it so that she didn't enjoy herself. Because once he got inside of her, it wouldn't take much for him to totally lose it. But she wanted more, and he was about to give it to her.

He removed his mouth, tracing kisses lower, over her flat stomach. As he knelt in front of her, his hands slid up her bared legs and beneath her skirt, where they stroked the curve of her ass. *Fuck.* He should've known she'd have a thong on.

Sofia reached behind her back and unzipped her skirt, letting it slip down lower. Dylan moved his hands so it could drop to the floor. Then he reached up and hooked his thumbs in either side of the strings across her hips, sliding down the thong. Sofia rested a hand on his shoulder as she stepped out of them, leaving her standing naked in front of him.

His mouth kissed and licked its way to her clit. He felt her shudder and her nails dug into his shoulder. "You taste so sweet," he muttered against her flesh.

"Dylan, please…I can't…" she said, her legs trembling.

He trailed kisses up again to claim her lips. Swiftly, never lifting his lips from hers, he picked her up and carried her down the hall to his bedroom. He laid her on the bed then quickly stripped off all his clothing, the buttons from his shirt echoed as they made contact with the hardwood floor. He could see her eyes roaming over him, taking in the view. Her tongue even darted out and she licked her lips as her eyes lingered over his cock. There was no way he was going to let her have a taste, because he was barely holding on now.

But before he could return to her, she was on her knees, reaching out to him. Her tongue darted out and licked him. *Fuck.* He knew he should push her away, but his body resisted. A low, husky growl echoed through the room and encouraged her to take more of him. His hands tangled in her long, dark hair, moving strays away from her face so he could watch as she licked him. She gripped his cock and took him fully into her mouth. *Oh fuck!* Her could feel her moans vibrating around him.

"God, baby, that feels so damn good." Dylan added, "Too good."

She hungrily took all he had to offer, sucking him deeply. Her tongue pressed firmly against his base to the head before circling and taking him in again, sucking harder and faster than the time before.

Dylan pulled away from her quickly, before it was too late. His cock was throbbing and close to release. Huskily, he said, "I don't want this to end before it even starts. And I want to taste you again."

Sofia didn't resist, and lay back on the bed. Her confidence in the bedroom was a fucking major turn-on. When he joined her on the bed, Dylan parted her legs with one hand, giving him full access. His mouth quickly devoured her and her cries echoed through the room when his tongue first touched her clit. He used his tongue to tease while his strong hands clenched her ass, pulling her up closer to him. One hand slid around, and he dipped a finger into her hot core. He could feel her tighten around him.

"You're so wet," he said against her folds. Once again, she tightened around his finger. As he entered her again, it didn't take long to find the spot inside that made her quiver and rock her hips. Using his thumb, he stroked her clit faster and faster, until he felt the waves of her climax take over and her body tense.

He whispered, "You don't know how badly I want to feel you wrapped around me." He pulled away slightly but wrapped her legs around him, trying to hold her in place. "Sweetheart, I just need to get a condom."

Only then did she release her hold. He reached out to the nightstand, opened the drawer, and pulled out a gold foil packet. He sheathed himself, then returned to kneel between her legs.

"Please," she begged.

Once he looked into her smoldering, lustful eyes, he entered her in a swift thrust. *Yes!* He knew exactly how to please her and positioned himself so he stroked her G-spot with each thrust. Quickly, another climax shook her.

As her moans filled the room, he found it impossible to contain his own. He stopped briefly to adjust his position, so her hips lifted from the bed, before he thrust deep within her again. He knew when to take them forward and when to pause long enough for the intensity to heighten. Sensing her need for more, he went even deeper and faster to bring her to climax a third time. But this time, Dylan couldn't hold back.

His own release shook him as he erupted into an explosive wave.

His body trembled, and sweat dripped from his head. That was fucking mind-blowing, and he was spent. Collapsing beside her, he rolled onto his back. Dylan pulled her so she rolled half onto him. With their legs entwined, breathing slowing, they lay holding each other.

Dylan could barely think, and his entire body seemed to have been drained of all energy. What the hell just happened? He'd been with many women, but never had a reaction like this. It more powerful than he'd ever imagined anything could be. And Sofia was so responsive to his touch that he figured she was feeling the same.

She stirred in his arms and said, "That was...amazing."

"I'm not going to argue with you on that."

"But we better get to sleep. Tomorrow is my first day on the job, and I don't want to go into work with bags under my eyes."

Dylan laughed. "Funny you mention that. I scheduled you to meet with HR tomorrow after lunch."

Sofia lifted her head off his chest and looked at him. "You mean I *don't* have to be up bright and early tomorrow?"

"Nope. Why?"

"Well, I haven't finished my research."

"Research?" he asked.

"Yes, on which bed I want to sleep in? What if the other one is more comfortable?"

"Oh, I think you're right." He rolled over and got up, then bent and scooped her up into his arms. "I'm not sure, the couch might need testing too."

She giggled. "I think we might need to try everything more than once, just to confirm our findings."

"Fuck."

"What's wrong?" Sofia asked.

"I should've had you start next week instead, because this is a big apartment."

"Then I guess we better get started," Sofia said as she nipped his neck.

I am so cancelling my meetings tomorrow.

13

Bacon? That wasn't a smell Dylan was used to waking up to. He knew there wasn't any in his house, so how the hell could it be possible? It couldn't, which meant sadly, he was still sleeping. It was a damn good dream though, Sofia cooking him breakfast and delivering it to him in bed. Of course, she would be naked when she brought him his tray. No matter how good the food smelled, he'd rather have her for breakfast.

Rolling over onto his back, he stretched and noticed the soft body that had been next to him wasn't there. Odd that he'd miss it after only being together for one night. But when he did eventually succumb to sleep, it was probably the best he'd had in a long time. Holding her in his arms, Sofia cuddled up against him, lightly snoring, almost like a purr in his ear. It was something he easily could get used to.

"If you don't get up, you're going to be late."

He lifted his head to see Sofia standing in the doorway dressed for the day. How the hell did she pull that off without him noticing? Maybe it'd been the lack of sleep for days that had wiped him out. But at least he had plenty of energy for what was important last night. *And I'm hoping for a replay this morning.*

"What's that smell?" he asked.

"Breakfast."

"Did you have it delivered?" Dylan asked.

She smiled and said, "No, I cooked it."

That had his attention. He sat up and leaned against the headboard. "I have to admit, you surprise me in many ways, but cooking what we don't have, well, that's a trick I wasn't prepared for."

"Don't worry. I didn't wave a magic wand or blink and make it all appear."

"Then please, tell me the secret to getting such wonderful-smelling food here without leaving the building."

Sofia leaned against the doorjamb, arms crossed, and said, "Easy, I asked your neighbors if I could borrow some. By the way, I promised to pick up a replacement on the way back tonight."

Dylan stared at her. There's no way he'd heard correctly. "You did what exactly?"

"I went down a floor, knocked on the doors, Peggy and John, very nice people by the way. And I asked if they had any breakfast items I could borrow. They hooked me up nicely, too. I have eggs, juice, toast, and that heavenly smell is—"

"Bacon," Dylan added. He didn't even know who lived in the building, and he'd been there for five years. One night and she was already knocking on doors?

"I can't believe you did that," he said.

"What did you expect me to do? I was hungry and the only thing you had besides coffee and alcohol, was a package of cookies."

He watched her hold up two chocolate cookies with white cream centers, then pop them both in her mouth.

"I can't believe you did that," Dylan said.

She chewed her food then said, "Borrow from your neighbors?"

"That too. But I meant fit those two cookies in your mouth like that. You're so…tiny."

She smirked. "I had no problem fitting you last night." Then she gave him a playful wink and his body instantly reacted.

Don't I know it.

"Sofia, if you keep this up, neither of us is making it to work today," he warned. Not that he cared. Grayson Corp. really didn't need him, and Rosslyn, although she was supposed to be on maternity leave, was still responding to all emails.

"Oh, I'm not missing my first day."

"I'm the boss, remember? We can go when we want," Dylan said.

"And that means you should be prompt, now if you want that breakfast, you're going to have to get up and get it," Sofia teased.

"Cracking the whip, are you?"

Sofia said, "Oh, sounds kinky, but if you want I'll—"

"No," he said. He pulled off the sheet and stood there naked. "I'm coming."

Her eyes roamed down him and smiled. "Without me?" she joked.

"Nope, and not before you either," he replied. "Why don't you come over here and I'll prove it to you?"

"Tonight, after food shopping, because I also promised Peggy and John I'd make them dinner later this week as a thank you. You know, this place isn't so bad after all…"

She smiled on the way out of the bedroom, leaving him alone, and in shock. She was already meeting people; if he wasn't careful, she'd have him doing the same. Dylan never socialized with the people here, except the security or maintenance staff. If it were up to him, he'd keep it that way. Somehow, he knew that was going to be impossible with Sofia around.

He hated it, but was going to need to have a talk with her. They might be living together, but he was set in his ways. And he didn't want to change. He knew it was going to spoil the lovely breakfast she'd prepared, but it had to be said. The earlier the better. *Hell, I should've said it before asking her to live with me.*

When he finally arrived in the kitchen, Sofia was standing at the sink, washing the dishes and humming to herself. She was…happy. That's all that really mattered to him. If it meant him having to get to know his neighbors, even when he didn't want to, then so be it. Because seeing her like this was all he cared about.

She turned around and said, "I hope you like it."

I do. Very much.

It wasn't the breakfast he was thinking about. It was having her there with him. Sofia might not have a magic wand, but whatever it was, it was unexplainable. She made everything feel…right, as though this was the way it was meant to be. He could get used to this so easily. But getting comfortable with something that wasn't going to last, wasn't smart. Once the play was over, this would be too. She'd either go back home, or with any luck, she'd get the break she'd been dreaming of. *At least for now, I can enjoy that beautiful smile every morning.*

. . .

Sofia was so nervous. She'd met Rosslyn before, but she hadn't been working for her then. But Dylan said he had to stop at her house to pick up a signed contract. She thought for sure he'd have left her in the car, but instead, he asked her to go in with him.

She realized right away that Charles and Rosslyn's home was much different from Dylan's. It had a more laid-back, homey feel to it. Maybe it was the baby swing and bassinette in the living room, but it made her feel so much more at ease.

"Hi Sofia, so nice to see you again. Sorry I didn't get to say goodbye last time," Rosslyn said.

Sofia chuckled. "I think you going into labor during dinner was probably a good excuse."

"Maria really called it, too. I can't believe she picked the day my little Penelope was going to be born."

"Mama does have that knack."

"Bet she can't wait for it to be your turn," she said.

"Oh, she'll be waiting a long time then. I'm in no rush," Sofia said firmly. A baby would change everything. Her dreams would have to be put on hold for eighteen years. *Might as well just give up on it then.* Nope. Having a family wasn't in her cards.

"If you and I were having this conversation about a year and a half ago, I'd tell you straight out, I'm not staying in New York City for anything. Look at me now. I'm married, with a baby, living in Manhattan." Rosslyn looked over to Charlie, who was holding their daughter. "I wouldn't change a thing."

Charlie said, "Well I was hoping you'd want to change one. Your daughter's diaper."

Rosslyn laughed. "Charles, it's not that bad."

He shook his head. "For a girl, she can stink up a room

THE BILLIONAIRE'S CHARADE

like a grown man." Dylan laughed and he added, "Maybe Uncle Dylan wants to give it a shot?"

"Hell no! I'm here for the contract, that's it."

Both women shot Dylan a look and Rosslyn warned, "Language."

Sofia watched as Charlie and Dylan nodded. She found it amusing how a little girl, not even ten pounds, was changing the Lawson family. But she was adorable.

"She's beautiful," Sofia said.

"Thanks. But she looks just like her mother," Charlie replied. Rosslyn grinned. Then he added, "Want to hold her?"

"Charles!" Rosslyn snapped. "That's horrible."

At first, Sofia thought Rosslyn didn't want strangers holding their baby. That really was a smart thing to do. They didn't know her, not really, after all. But then she realized that wasn't the case.

"You can't blame me for trying," Charlie said with a grin.

"Oh yes I can." Rosslyn got up and took Penelope from Charlie, then turned to Sofia. "If you can sit for a bit, I'll only be a few minutes. Once she's all clean, she'll be in a better mood to be held."

Before Sofia could decline and say they were on their way to the office, Rosslyn was already on her way to the nursery, singing as she walked.

Dylan whispered, "That was close."

Sofia turned to him and said, "I love children. I'm not afraid to hold them."

"I'm talking about the diaper."

"Really? You Lawson men are a force to be reckoned with in the business world, but a dirty diaper scares you?" Neither disputed it. Rolling her eyes, she said, "I guess everyone has their kryptonite."

"I wouldn't go that far," Dylan said.

"I would," Charlie added. "Trust me, you'll understand when you have your own children."

There seemed to be a lot of talk of children going on. Did they think there was more happening between her and Dylan than there was? Heck, she wasn't even sure if they knew she was staying with him. *And I'm not about to share that info, either.*

"Who is having a baby?" Gareth said from behind them. When they all looked at him he added, "Sorry, I knocked but no one answered. So I let myself in. Did I interrupt a private conversation? Maybe something you're not ready to share with the rest of the family?" He winked at Dylan.

"Don't look at me like that. You're next in line, buddy," Dylan said.

Gareth asked, "What is that line? Oh yeah. First comes love, second comes marriage, then comes—"

"Knock it off Gareth," Dylan warned.

"Hey, I figure since you two are living together, then it's got to be pretty serious," Gareth added.

"Living together? Really?" Rosslyn said with a look of joy on her face. "How come no one told me?" She shot her husband a questioning look.

"I didn't know either," Charlie defended. "Seems the dark circles under my brother's eyes aren't from you overworking him at Grayson Corp. after all."

Sofia wished she could sneak out of the room and go back in the car. She could tell by the expression on Dylan's face, he wasn't enjoying this banter either. Maybe he really didn't want people knowing about them being together. But were they? Together? Hot, passionate, mind-blowing sex didn't mean they were in a relationship. Living together didn't either, but it wasn't *their* place, it was his. She needed to fix this before it got out of hand.

"Sorry, but you guys have it all wrong. Dylan and I are not involved. He's just helping me out while I work in the city. That's all. Nothing more. When the job is done, which hopefully will only be a few months, I will be on to the next one."

Was it her imagination, or did Dylan flinch? The entire room seemed to have gotten quiet as well. The awkward silence was deafening.

"I hope we didn't make you feel…uncomfortable with our…assumption. It's just that…well…it appeared to be more. But I'm glad you clarified it for us," Rosslyn said, now back in the room with a clean baby.

Sofia could feel all eyes on her except for Dylan's. He seemed to be looking anywhere but at her. Had she spoken out of line? She was trying to help. From the look on everyone's face, it had worked. Dylan should look relieved that the talk of them having a baby was now history.

I don't get it. You just can't make a man happy.

Forcing a smile, she replied, "No harm. I can see how it easily could be misconstrued to appear as more."

Gareth blurted, "I'm not buying it. I know my brother."

Dylan shot him a look that could kill. "You heard her. It's nothing." Then he turned to Rosslyn and said, "I'll review the contract and get it sent out today. If there are any questions, or changes, I'll let you know."

Sofia could feel the fumes coming from him. If she noticed it, the others, who knew him even better, surely picked up on it. But she kept her composure and kept quiet. *Something I should've done before.*

The light, fun mood from before, gone. They said their goodbyes and were on their way to the office. Should she confront him now about what had just happened? Would that make it worse? She didn't see how it could. But what did she know? Nothing about them was anything like what she'd been through before. From their initial meeting, things were...unique. But at no point had either of them classified what this was between them.

She knew she'd avoided it herself because it wasn't what she'd planned. Did she care for him? More than she'd ever expected to. Maybe to the point that she was falling in love with him. That definitely wasn't part of her plan. And from the looks of his bachelor pad, love wasn't something he was looking for either. *And he never said he loved me, anyway.*

So, from her point of view, he should be thanking her, not giving her the silent treatment. *But then again, I might not want to hear what he has to say, either.*

No. She wasn't going to ask. They were on their way to work, a place where you shouldn't bring your personal drama. If things were still tense between them tonight, then maybe she'd ask. *Or maybe I won't have to, and he'll just tell me what the hell I did wrong.*

It was going to be one hell of a long-ass day. The good news was, she didn't work directly for him. After her meeting with HR, she should be able to find numerous things to keep her mind off him. *Who am I fooling? I'm not going to be able to focus on shit until we talk.*

She caught sight of him out of the corner of her eye. Now definitely wasn't the time. Hopefully a few hours apart would have defused what really shouldn't even have been an issue, and they could go back to the way things were before she'd opened her big mouth.

As she had expected, the day was about as smooth as her morning had been. HR didn't seem to have any of her information correct, which was probably because she'd never completed an application. They had expected her to have her resume on hand as well, which she didn't have prepared.

'Waitress since sixteen' wasn't really going to make her look qualified for the position. There was nothing like a reminder that she hadn't gotten this job on her own merit. That only made her feel worse about what had happened between her and Dylan. He'd done so much for her, and she'd embarrassed him in front of his family.

Between her meeting with HR, and the fact that she'd blown her rehearsal last night, there was only one thing keeping her in the city, and that was Dylan. And now, she may have screwed that up, too. Granted, Grayson Corp. was a large building, but she'd thought for sure she would've heard from him at some point. Yet, not one word. If she couldn't fix this, then maybe it was time she faced the facts. New York City was a dream, but Mama's Place was her reality. Was it time for her to pack up again and go home with her tail tucked between her legs? At least she could say she tried her best.

That wasn't true at all. Even now, as she left the second day of rehearsal, she still didn't feel good about it. Although the director hadn't spent the entire night yelling at her, nothing positive was said, either. Probably because another actor had felt his wrath tonight. Sofia could empathize with them, as it was a public lashing, for all to see. By the time you left the theater, your self-worth and confidence had been effectively chipped away at. If you returned after that, you had to be a glutton for punishment. The only good thing about the day was, it was coming to an end.

She wanted nothing more than to go back to the apartment, get into a hot bath, and forget all about today. But she couldn't soak away the issues between her and Dylan. With any luck, he'd be there and waiting for her.

Wishing for flowers would be hoping for way too much, but then again, I always did dream big.

But when she arrived, he wasn't there. The doorman was there as usual, waiting to open the private elevator to the penthouse for her. Once she got inside, she sent him a text message.

WILL YOU BE COMING HOME? She read it back and then deleted it. This was his home, not theirs. So she typed again. IS EVERTHING OKAY?

She hit send, but then wished she hadn't. Was it any of her business? Was she worried? Yes. That didn't change anything. So she tossed her phone on the kitchen counter and went into the bathroom. There was nothing she could do about it unless he was willing to talk. And since he hadn't responded to her text, she assumed things were the way he'd left them. *Maybe they always will be.*

After her suck-ass day and running on little sleep, she dozed off in the tub. The water was cold and so was she. But more importantly, she could hear swearing coming from another part of the house. She climbed out of the bathtub, grabbed a towel, and twisted it around her hair. Then she took a bath sheet and covered herself, being sure to tuck it in tightly before going out to see what the commotion was.

When she arrived in the kitchen, she saw the center island counter cluttered with brown paper shopping bags, but no one was in sight. Someone was there.

Another round of curses echoed through the room, but she knew its origin. Walking around the counter, she found Dylan kneeling on the floor with paper towels.

He looked up at her, then back to the floor. "What the fuck? These paper towels are supposed to pick up anything."

She held back her laughter, then knelt down and took the paper towels from him. "Eggs are a bitch to pick up. Why don't you let me do that?"

"No, I can do it," he said.

"But I have more experience." He looked at her, doubtful, so she added, "Trust me. I have dropped more eggs than I'll ever admit to my mother."

He laughed. "Okay. You handle this, and I'll try to put the rest away without dropping anything."

She scooped up the raw eggs but hoped this would be a good time to talk. *Start slow.* "So what's all this?"

"Food."

Duh. "I mean, why so much?"

"Not all of it is ours. Some belongs to...what are their names?" Dylan asked.

"Peggy and John?"

"Yeah, them. I think I have everything you borrowed. Well, I did." He pointed at the empty carton of eggs. "Guess you're going to have to give them another IOU."

She giggled. "I'm sure they will have no problem with that if I deliver the news with a promise of some homemade cookies."

Dylan paused. "I shopped. Like a guy. Basics only."

She got up and looked through the bags. Bread. Milk. Juice. Peanut butter. Jelly. "Please don't tell me you bought frozen dinners?" She took out the box that looked like some kind of meat, with what was supposed to be potatoes.

"I wasn't sure what you'd want."

"I would've gone and picked it up, but I was hoping that..."

"Hoping what?" he asked.

"That you'd be here and we could talk about what happened at Charlie's house." He looked away and pretended to be unpacking food. She was beginning to be able to tell the difference now. "Should I start by saying I'm sorry?"

He shook his head. "No. I should. I was the one who put you in that situation. My family can be..."

181

"Presumptuous?"

"Pains in the ass is more like it. Gareth likes to joke around a lot and Rosslyn, well, I think because she's a mother now, she wants one of us to have one right away. You know, someone for Penelope to grow up with."

"That's kind of sweet. But that doesn't explain why you became so...quiet. Because it sounds like you expected that behavior from them."

He looked at her for what seemed like an eternity. When he spoke, his words were like a knife. "I did. It was yours that...hurt."

"Mine? What did I say?" She really didn't recall anything that horrible.

"Nothing."

"I don't understand. You said it was what I said." She was totally confused.

"Yes. You said nothing and used that word more than once. There is nothing between us. Nothing. Is that how you really feel, Sofia?"

She could see now that her choice to conceal their relationship had been the wrong one. "No. Not at all. When I realized they didn't know you were allowing me to stay here, I figured you didn't want anyone to know."

"I don't share my business or ask their permission. Besides, it hadn't come up, and we've been a bit preoccupied. Or had you forgotten that as well?"

She deserved that. 'Sorry' didn't seem to be anywhere near enough of an apology. The damage was done, and now his family believed they were...*nothing* to each other. "What can I say Dylan, to make this...right?"

He came around the counter and looked directly into her eyes. "The truth."

"To your family?" she asked.

Dylan shook his head. "I don't give a damn what they believe. I want you to tell *me*. Why are you here, Sofia?"

"You offered me the job, and I'm in the play, and—"

"And if you were fired from both? What is left for you, Sofia? Anything, or *nothing?*"

How could she tell him what she wasn't sure of herself? "Dylan, I care so much about you and I'm…I…I don't want it to end. I just don't know what *this* is. We've never talked about it."

"You're right. We started, but got…distracted. So why don't we talk now?"

"Okay." *You go first.*

"Let me start by saying, I didn't ask you to come here for any damn job. Or because of a play, for that matter."

"Why did you ask me then?"

"Because I wanted to see more of you. The way we were going, neither of us was getting any sleep. Of course, I don't remember sleeping much last night, but at least we were together."

"Yes, we are. But as what? Lovers?"

"I would say we are definitely lovers. But I want to think we are more than just that. Did you see how I live here? It has been a bachelor pad. No other woman has ever been here. I liked it that way." He tipped her chin and asked, "Do you understand what I'm saying?"

"Yes. You like living alone. You like being single." It was crystal clear.

"No, sweetheart, I said 'liked'. That is the past. This is what I want right now. You. Me. Here."

They weren't words professing his love, and she wasn't ready to do that, either. But at least she knew she wasn't his flavor-of-the-month gal. "So where do we go from here?"

"Honestly Sofia, I don't know. This is all new to me. I

know it's asking a lot, but I'm hoping we can take our time and figure this out together."

He was right. There was no reason to rush into defining or labeling their relationship. There was still so much for them to learn about each other. She didn't even know his favorite color or food. From what she'd seen, he pretty much ate whatever there was. But that wasn't enough to decide a future. And he didn't know hers, either. She came to the city with the intention of leaving when the play finished. It was possible that in eight weeks she might have had her fill of being here, even if she still enjoyed being with him.

"I think it's a great idea."

"Good. Then maybe, if it's okay with you, we can... invite...what are their names again?"

"Peggy and John."

"Yes, Peggy and John over for dinner this weekend to say thanks for the food. That is, if you're in the mood for company and for cooking."

She couldn't hold back her excitement. "I'd really like that."

"And I thought maybe a few others. Kind of make it a dinner party."

"Okay. I know how to cook enough to feed an army." She really did. Hopefully that wasn't how many he was inviting. "About how many people?"

"I was thinking the usual. My family. Maybe yours, if you'd like, and even Charlene if you think she'd come."

Sofia pulled away for a moment and looked at him. This was great, but it didn't seem right. Something was off. "Dylan, I know I'm agreeing to all this, but now I'm not so sure. Why are you doing this?"

"Because I want you to feel like this isn't just my place.

That you live here too. I know having people around is important to you."

She could kiss him. Once again, he was doing something to make her happy. Sofia knew she could jump at the chance and invite them all. But the last thing she wanted was either of them changing who they were for the other person. So she reached out and took his hand in hers. "Then I guess I have to say no."

"To living here?"

She shook her head. "I don't want to be anywhere else. I'm talking about having the party. You wanting me to feel at home will only work if we both do. So let's start small. Pick someone and I'll cook. Make it casual, and then they can go home early."

He pulled her into his arms. "So we can be alone and really enjoy the place."

Sofia smiled. "I'll even make a special dessert for us to share."

"In bed?" he teased.

"Anywhere you want to eat it," she said seductively.

"Hmmm. Can I have a sample now?" he asked.

"I haven't made it?" she replied.

"You're the only dessert I desire." Dylan reached between them and tugged the towel. She felt it break loose and drop to the floor. "I don't believe we've done any *research* in the kitchen yet."

"Then maybe we should get cooking." Sofia reached up and loosened his tie as her lips touched his.

Definitely my favorite dessert too.

"Charlene, it's not an easy decision."

"It sounds like it to me. But then again, you always like to micro-analyze everything," Charlene replied. "Can you just admit that you're happy with how things are?"

"But what about my dreams? I've wanted this for so long."

"Yeah. So?"

Charlene didn't get it. For years, all she'd wanted was to score a good role. Now that the opportunity had presented itself, she wasn't sure she wanted it. "Do you know you're absolutely no help at all?"

"You could call your mother. But I'm sure you're going to hear the same thing."

She was right. Mama was going to tell her a career wasn't as important as a husband. But she wasn't married. Actually, they hadn't even spoken of marriage. They'd been living together for four months and things were going so smoothly that she couldn't be happier. Well, there was one thing that she'd change, and that was how many hours they spent apart. It was one drawback to being part of a production. With the hours involved, it was like working another full-time job.

"Mama just wants grandchildren. She'd say anything to get them. Why don't you marry Sal and give her some, so she'll leave me alone?" Sofia teased.

"Gross. Sal is so…by the book."

"He's a police officer. What do you want?" Sofia asked.

"Adventure. You know, someone who doesn't mind living on the edge once in a while. Someone who can skinny dip on a whim."

Sofia rolled her eyes. If Sal did skinny dip, she didn't want to know about it. "Charlene, I was joking. I love you as my best friend, but you could never survive having Mama as your mother-in-law."

"Oh God no. I forgot all about that. Sal is off the list." Charlene laughed. "So, I guess that means you'll just have to give her a son-in-law."

"Since when did you start siding with her?" Sofia asked.

"Well, with you in the city, I have to go in and get my own meals. That means your mother spends her time asking me all these questions, instead of you. The only thing that's going to make her stop is you getting married."

So you think. "I guess you have two choices."

"What are they?" Charlene asked.

"Either make your answers shorter so she stops or find another place to eat."

"Wait, I was getting excited. I already picked out my maid-of-honor dress too."

"You'll be in a wedding dress before you're my maid of honor. Dylan and I are happy just the way we are. Why screw with it? Do you know how many relationships work until they get married?" Sofia really didn't have any numbers on it, but she remembered hearing it somewhere.

"Wow. You're really scared," Charlene said. "I thought it was the acting thing that was holding you back, but it's not. It's...you."

"What are you talking about?"

"Sofia, besties know this shit. This has nothing to do with a career, your mother or even Dylan. You're questioning yourself."

"Really? Did you get a degree in psychology that I'm unaware of?"

"And your reluctance to talk about it only proves how right I am. So, do I need to come up there and give you a lecture in person, or can I do it over the phone? Because you're getting one whether you like it or not."

She questioned why she'd even bothered calling Charlene. It definitely wasn't to hear this crap. Sofia wasn't afraid of being with Dylan. Actually, she looked forward to going home each night to his waiting arms.

"What can I say to make you stop?"

Charlene said, "Three words."

"Which are?"

"I love you," Charlene said firmly.

That's simple. "Okay. I love you."

Charlene let out an exasperated sigh. "I'm glad you're taking this seriously," she said sarcastically.

"Don't you think my feelings for Dylan are between him and me?"

"I do. Have you told him that you love him?"

No. "Charlene, he knows how I feel."

"Is that a yes?"

Damn it girl. If it wasn't for the fact that she loved Charlene like a sister, she'd probably have hung up by now.

"No. I haven't said it outright. But I'm sure he knows how I feel."

"Okay, so has he said it?" Charlene asked.

"No. But before you ask, I know how he feels too." Not really, but hopefully that would be enough to appease Charlene.

"Why don't you tell him tonight? Make him a romantic dinner, candles and everything, and then tell him you love him."

"And why don't you mind your business? I know how to handle my own relationship."

"Good. Then I expect a call tomorrow so you can tell me how it went. Now go out and buy yourself something sexy to wear too. Oh, how about something fun, like black leather chaps and—"

"Charlene, I've got to go. Work is calling."

"I didn't hear a beep," Charlene said.

Sofia laughed and said, "Beep. Did you hear it now?"

"You're so lucky I love you."

"I know. And trust me Charlene, I appreciate having you in my life more than you know." Sofia knew no matter what she chose to do, Charlene would be there. It might come with a hell of a lot of ribbing, but it was better than having a dull, lifeless friend.

When the call ended, Sofia was left more confused as to what to do than before. She hadn't even told Dylan about the offer for the lead role. Not because she was afraid he wouldn't support her, but because she really didn't know what she wanted anymore.

When did it become so complex?

Back at Mama's Place, she never had to worry about anything like this. The only changes were to the special of the day on the menu. Besides that, everything was predictable. That wasn't her life right now. And taking Charlene's advice and telling Dylan how she felt, was one thing she wanted to be able to predict the outcome of.

If she went with her gut, then Dylan would tell her how much he loved her too, they'd kiss and end up in bed making sweet love all night long. There were no indicators to show anything but it being welcomed. So why hadn't she already told him?

Maybe Charlene was right and she was afraid of taking the next step. It made no sense because nothing would change, but in her heart, it would. She'd never told anyone that she loved them. Until recently, she never thought about it. There were people she'd dated and cared about, but she'd never been in love, the kind that made you think about the future.

That's what she was doing. Thinking of all the changes so far in such a short amount of time was overwhelming. Not just for her either, but Dylan had opened his home to her when he enjoyed being alone. But they were on the same page back then, neither looking for this to go beyond where they were. It was clear that marriage and children were not in either of their cards. Or at least, they hadn't been.

Sofia had spent her day at the doctor, because she was late and her first thought was, she was pregnant. But the blood work returned negative and the doctor determined it was due to stress. At first, she was so relieved to hear the report. Stress she could manage on her own, but a baby would be something she'd need to talk to Dylan about. But as the day went on, she was faced with a different revelation, one she hadn't expected. A sadness about the test results.

It wasn't that she wanted to be a mother right now, but if that had been the case, she would've embraced it with love. That's when she realized she may have changed more than

Dylan. For the first time, she was actually thinking about having her own family someday.

That's why she'd held back telling Dylan she loved him. Because if she was going that far, shouldn't she also tell him everything? They promised to always be open and honest with each other. But she also knew Dylan would do anything to make her happy. No matter how many times she told him no, if it brought a smile to her face, he did it.

She was spoiled, not with gifts, because they meant nothing to her, but with time and romance. If she mentioned wanting a family, she feared he'd give her one, but for the wrong reasons. She wanted him to want children just as much as she did. Right now, she wasn't sure that was accurate.

Could she continue being with him if he didn't want any children? *Would he run if he knew that I did?*

Sofia wasn't about to risk it all just to find out.

As though Dylan knew she was thinking about him, he called.

"Hi Sofia. Do you have any plans for this weekend that I'm not aware of?"

"No. With Rosslyn back to work, and between gigs, I'm free. Was there something you'd like to do?"

"Yes."

She waited for him to say more, but he didn't. "Well that's not much to go on. Should we play the game twenty questions?"

"No."

Again, the one-word answers. Well, it wasn't her birthday, so that wasn't it. And no holiday either. She had no clue what he was up to.

"Dylan, I really don't like surprises, so why don't you just tell me what's going on?"

He laughed. "You don't like them, but you sure like to do it to me all the time."

"I don't know what you're talking about." That wasn't true. She liked making special meals for him or having candles and a bubble bath waiting for them with strawberries and champagne. He did romantic things too, but usually told her. So why was he holding back now?

"Sofia, I'm not telling you anything," he said firmly.

"I'm not sure I like this," Sofia said.

"You're just going to have to wait. And nothing you say is going to get me to spill it."

So you think. I have my ways. She'd turn up the charm tonight and see if he caved. The playfulness was just the distraction she needed to break up her deep thoughts. But it also made her want to beat him to the punch. *I wonder if assless leather chaps, some nipple pasties, and a whip would do the trick?* Even thinking about her dressed like that brought her to tears of laughter. She'd let him have this one, but the next, is all hers.

Dylan knew it was cruel, but he knew Sofia would be going crazy trying to figure out what he had planned. What she never would've guessed was who his ally was. Charlene had proven to be invaluable when it came to pulling it all together. Of course, working with her was a different story. Charlene was a lot more high-strung than Dylan could deal with for long periods of time. But if it meant surprising Sofia, then he'd suffer through it.

He picked up the phone and called to confirm everything was going as planned.

"Please don't tell me you're checking up on me again?" Charlene said.

Someone's got to. "I just got off the phone with Sofia. She has no clue."

"Of course not. I spoke to her for more than an hour and didn't even drop one hint."

With how much Charlene talked, he was surprised by that. "Good. I'm picking her up for dinner tonight as usual."

"So I heard from Sofia."

"I'm counting on you, Charlene."

"I might be a blonde, but I'm very capable of following instructions, so quit hounding me like I'm stupid."

"Sorry. This is just very important to me."

"Gee, I can't tell. But if you don't relax, she's going to figure it out."

"No way."

"You're not giving her enough credit. Even as kids, if she wanted to know something, nothing stopped her from finding the answer. So I hope you didn't give her a reason to go looking."

Fuck! "You would think you'd give me that kind of info up front."

Charlene laughed. "Dylan, when I tried warning you, I believe you said you had everything under control."

"And I do." *Or at least I did.* He was worried right now. Sofia was home and had too much time on her hands. If Charlene was right, he might have just blown it.

"Okay, well then all I can say is good luck."

I hope I don't need it. "Thanks."

He ended the call and slipped the phone into the breast pocket of his jacket. Everything was set. In a few hours, he'd know if he'd played this correctly. God, he hoped so. He really believed this was what she wanted. What would make her happy.

A few contracts later, Dylan called it a day. He couldn't

wait to pick up Sofia. This was going to be a night she would never forget.

When he opened the door to the apartment, she was dressed and ready for dinner, or so she thought.

She greeted him with a kiss and said, "I'm starving. Where are we going tonight?"

"It's a ways off."

"You mean it's not in the city?"

"It is, but the wait can be long." Lying to her didn't come easily.

"Okay. We can talk while waiting."

Before long, they were in the limo and pulling up to a small restaurant. This was it. Once inside, the secret would be revealed. She'd made it clear she didn't like surprises, and this was one hell of one. Either she'd be ecstatic or pissed.

"Are you ready?"

"Starving, but it doesn't look like there's a line. Actually, it almost looks like it's closed."

"It's open," he said. *For a private party only.*

She stopped. "Dylan, I know food, and if a place is empty on a Friday night, you shouldn't eat there."

"Trust me. The place has a great reputation," he said, urging her forward.

She took a few steps then stopped again. "We can always go to Mama's Place. You'll never guess what the special is tonight. One of your favorites."

Nothing was getting him to turn around now. It took a lot of planning to get this set up. Granted, he could try again another time, but he was used to getting what he wanted, when he wanted it.

"We can go there tomorrow. But we're here now."

"Okay, but if I get sick, I'm blaming you," she said.

You won't. When they got inside, the tables were empty,

194

all except for one. He guided her over and as soon as they got there, Sofia must have realized the surprise wasn't this week-end, it was tonight.

She turned to him and asked, "What's going on Dylan?"

"Sofia, a few months ago, I looked into those beautiful honey-brown eyes of yours and knew you were going to be trouble. I just didn't know how much. You took my world and turned it upside down. It needed some shaking. I just hadn't realized it before. But you seem to have derailed in the process. I remember the woman who was so driven that nothing stood in her way. Yet it seems that *I* got in your way. Your show, even though it was a hit, is over, and you're sitting home, spinning your wheels. I know life has another adventure in store for you. All you have to do, is grab the brass ring."

She looked around, then back to him. "What are you trying to say Dylan?"

"That I know you wouldn't do this, so I made the move for you. I believe you know Paully Jones, the director?"

"I do. What I don't know is, why is he here?"

"For your audition for a part in a movie," Dylan said. Dylan thought for a moment that she was about to faint and he stepped closer to give her a supportive arm.

"Movie? Me? How?" Sofia asked.

"I got a copy of your performance in the play and sent it to Mr. Jones. Then I asked him here to meet with you." There may have been more than just talking, like actual cash exchange, but she didn't need to know that.

"I don't know what to say?" Sofia said softly.

"You don't have to say anything, at least not to me. Mr. Jones has the information for you to read. The rest is all on you, sweetheart. I just opened the door. You have to decide if you want to walk through it."

He really expected her to be beaming the moment she saw Jones sitting there. He was a very well-known director and potentially could be the break Sofia had longed for. But she didn't look overjoyed as expected.

"What are you going to do while we talk?" Sofia asked.

"I'm going to go home, but I'm leaving the limo for you." He leaned over and kissed her then added, "Break a leg."

"Thank you, Dylan. This means a lot to me." Sofia turned and walked over to Jones. He wished he could stay and watch, but this was her moment to shine. And he knew she would. All she needed was for someone to put her back on her path. He knew once she started, she was going to take off and obtain all she had dreamed of. *And knowing she's happy is all that matters.*

Dylan never knew what love felt like, but he realized it is a selfless emotion. Her needs, wants, and desires came before his own.

It was odd how much he had changed since meeting her. But there were things that hadn't. He was still business-driven. If she took this job, then it was a good thing he had his work, because he was going to need to fill his time with something.

Damn it. I'm going to miss her like hell when she's gone. He knew Sofia was going to impress Jones. And the film wasn't going to be shot anywhere near New York. Actually, it wasn't even in the States. *Going big screen, sweetheart. And I know you'll rock it.*

15

Everything she had wanted was right there in front of her. But it was lacking what she wanted most. Even though Paully Jones said she aced her private audition, her heart wasn't in it. Dylan had left. This had all come about because of him and he was who she wanted to share her joy with.

"Mr. Jones, I really appreciate your offer. And the fact that you actually flew out here to meet with me is something I'll never forget. But the timing isn't right. Actually it's a bit late."

"You already are committed for another film?" he asked.

"No. But I do have another commitment. One that means the world to me."

He smiled. "Mr. Lawson is a lucky man. Not many women would give up an opportunity like this for love."

Love. That's exactly what was keeping her there. "Being with him is the role of a lifetime." And one she was working to prefect.

"If you change your mind, give me a call." He handed her his business card. "I can't promise you that the offer will still be available, but I have connections. I'm sure I can put in a good word for you."

"Thank you." She slipped the card into her purse and said, "If you don't mind, I'd like to tell Dylan myself."

"Of course." Pauly turned to leave the restaurant and Sofia was left standing there alone.

She wanted to rush right to Dylan and tell him she loved him. Yet how was she going to explain that he'd gone through all this effort for her and she just turned down the opportunity of a lifetime? Sofia didn't want to disappoint him, but she couldn't see any way around it. No matter what, it was as though she was backing down from everything she had said. She didn't want a family, now she does. She wanted to be a famous actress, now she doesn't. If she wasn't careful, the next thing would be she wanted to someday run Mama's Place. Even that thought didn't disturb her like it used too.

Once again, Sofia felt a bit lightheaded. She still hadn't eaten and that added onto everything else today, was more than she could take. So she headed for the limo and asked him to stop and get her a milk and some crackers on the way back home. She didn't even have the energy to get out and go into the store herself. She knew it would pass once she ate something. Even though she was hungry enough to eat an entire pizza herself, her nerves was playing havoc on her stomach and the last thing she wanted to do was hurl on Dylan while she was professing her love for him. She did say the next surprise was coming from her, but that wasn't how she wanted to present it.

When the limo driver returned and handed her the items she said, "Could I trouble you to do me one more favor?"

"It's no trouble at all. What do you need?"

"Flowers," she said.

"Is there any certain kind?" he asked.

She had no clue. What flower do you get a man when you want to say I love you? Sofia couldn't come up with anything. "Maybe we skip the flowers. I just need something, But I'm not sure exactly what."

"If you want to tell me what you're trying to do, then maybe I can offer a suggestion."

Although she had become accustom to having Dylan's driver take her around town, she wasn't so comfortable as to share her dilemma with him. She contemplated on calling Charlene, but that call would go on forever and by the end, it would be something absolutely ridiculous. Charlene was awesome, but she liked to get her freak on and was always trying to get Sofia to do the same. There was no problem with that, but this was not the occasion.

If she called her mother, that would be as good as putting it in the newspaper or heck, maybe even the national news. But her advice would be sound. She'd gotten to talk to Rosslyn many times over the last few months, but she had her hands full. Was the driver really her only option?

No. "I just need a few minutes to make a call and I'll let you know."

"Whenever you're ready miss." He rolled up the divider window as she pulled out her cell phone.

The timing for this was the worst. Friday nights were crazy busy, but this was important. Hopefully he was free to take her call. It rang a few times, but finally he answered.

"I thought you lost my number," Sal said when he answered.

"Phones work both ways you know."

"Who needs to call when I can get all the news I want from Mama and Charlene. Seems like things are going really good in Manhattan. I'm happy for you."

"Really Sal? Because I know in the beginning you

weren't thrilled I was dating Dylan." She never forgot that first family dinner together. It was tense.

"That's because something felt...off. But Charlene explained everything to me."

She what? "What exactly did she say?"

"That you were sneaking out to Manhattan at night because you were in a play and didn't have the balls to tell the folks. So you and Dylan concocted this stupid plan to look like a couple. Guess that didn't go as planned."

"What do you mean?" she asked.

He laughed. "You guys sucked at acting so you had to go for the real thing. Bet he never saw that coming. Of course you know who did?"

Mama. "Well I'm calling you for some advice."

"Or whether or not you should take that movie deal?" Sal said.

Her eyes widened. "How did you know?" She had just learned of it and hadn't said a word to anyone.

"Charlene told me."

"Charlene? How did she know?" Sofia was confused.

"Dylan told her. She told me. Guess she helped get things in order. You know, make sure you were free for dinner and stuff like that. I really don't know what she does. After a few minutes, I stop listening, if you know what I mean."

She did. So Dylan really wanted her to take this role. If not, he'd never would've reached out to Charlene for help. This made things even harder. Now how was she going to tell him she turned it down?

"Does Mama know too?" She crossed her fingers and waited.

"No. Charlene has been using me as her confidant in all this. Just so you know, I don't want to be your replacement in her life. Maybe you can visit her more often before she drives me nuts."

If there weren't a million things running through her mind already, she'd have some witty comebacks for him. But she needed to stay focused on her and Dylan at the moment.

"Sal, can you please do me a favor?"

"For you sis, anything."

"Don't tell anyone about the movie deal."

"Wouldn't dream of it. I leave the gossip to you ladies," he teased.

"You're lucky you're not here or I'd…" *hug you for being the best brother ever.*

"So you off to deliver the big news to Dylan?" Sal asked.

Even though he had set it all up, Sofia knew he'd be at home waiting to hear all about it. "I am."

"So what did you call me for? You never said."

And she wasn't about to any longer. "Just to say hi. And that I miss you. And love you."

"I love you too sis. And really, I'm very happy for you. It seems like everything you wanted is at your fingertips. That doesn't happen often in life."

"No it doesn't." For Sofia, it wasn't the movie, it was finding Dylan.

She ended the call and told the driver to take her home. Sofia didn't need flowers or a gift. It wasn't about romance right now. It was what was in her heart and telling him that she loved him was the best she could give him. *Since I'm jobless, it really is all I got right now.* Hopefully he'd understand that she appreciated all he's done, it's just that she had changed.

The ding announced the private elevator was coming up. That

meant Sofia would be home any second now. He had every-thing set up perfectly. The food looked fantastic, the flowers smelled great and it was time to celebrate. Unfortunately there was a part of him that didn't want to. Even when he left her with Paully Jones, it was as though they were parting ways. It was ridiculous because they could continue with their relationship, even from a distance. It just wouldn't be the same. And for once in his life, he was...content.

Dylan had always been searching for more. With Sofia, he had it all, what was left to want? She was the one that made this apartment a home. Without her here, it'd feel so... empty. He didn't want to go back to the way things were before. Why would you when you held a piece of heaven in your hands. Letting it go only hurt even more. But it was for the best, for her at least.

Remember, this is all about Sofia. Because he loved her so much, no way could he stand in her way and not let her be all she dreamt of being.

The room was quiet and he looked around. Everyone also knew the moment was coming. Soon the doors would open and she'd come out. Everyone would shout their cheers and she'd be swept up in all the excitement. Charlene did an amazing job with making sure everything was perfect while he brought Sofia for the meeting. And of course her parents had insisted on cooking the food and bringing it with them. He was glad they had. Sal seemed to be in deep conversation with Charles, but old friends needed to catch up when they could. It was perfect. The entire Lawson family was in atten-dance and the Marciano's as well. Hell, even their new friends Peggy and John came up for the big announcement.

He took a deep breath as he saw the doors begin to open. The moment she stepped out and into the apartment everyone shouted, "Congratulations!"

Sofia stopped cold in her tracks and had the deer in the headlights look. Dylan walked over and gave her a kiss on the cheek. "Surprise," he said softly.

She looked up at him and asked, "What is all this? Why is everyone here?"

"To celebrate with you. Everyone is so happy for you." *Even me in my own way.* Sofia grabbed hold of his forearm and swayed. He put an arm around her waist to support her. "Are you okay?"

"Yes. I still haven't really eaten anything. And now I'm not sure I could. Dylan, you did all this for me?"

"Yes, but I had help. As you can see, decorations were handled by Charlene, and food by your parents and flowers by Rosslyn. But I handled the guest list. I knew this night was important to you and you'd want to shout out to the world. So I brought our world here." He was having a hard time reading her. Her lips curled, but the smile wasn't genuine. Had he played this wrong. Did she want to tell people herself? *Of course, dumbass. This was her news, not mine.* It was too late to fix that now.

She said, "This is all very nice."

Nice. Great. He could tell just by holding her that she wasn't comfortable with this. Dylan had no problem telling everyone to leave, but they weren't going to go willingly. Everyone in this room loved Sofia and wanted to be here for her.

Charlene came over and gave her a quick side hug. Dylan wasn't removing his arm from supporting her for anything. Even if she didn't need him, he needed to hold her. It wouldn't be long before he couldn't any more.

"I'm so happy for you." Then she whispered in Sofia's ear but Dylan could still hear. "Glad you didn't come in wearing the leather chaps."

Dylan looked down at Sofia who blushed.

"Charlene, you're horrible. But thanks for coming and thank you for doing this with Dylan. It means so much to me." Sofia's eyes were watering.

He knew this would be an emotional time, and he was prepared. He pulled out a tissue from his pocket and handed it to her. "I know, it's been a crazy night, and it seems like it's going to get even more so."

Charlene cheered, "Speech. Speech. Speech."

Sofia glanced at her and then up to Dylan. "I need to talk to you."

"Now?"

She looked around the room while nodding. Her mother approached and said, "My daughter the movie star."

Dylan felt her tense as she said, "No Mama. I'm not. I turned down the role."

Maria looked shocked but nothing compared to how Dylan felt. "You what?"

She turned and looked up at him again. "Dylan, I can't thank you enough for getting Paully Jones to come out to meet with me. No one has ever done anything like that before. It really showed me how much you listen when I talk. You really understood what my dreams were."

"I thought I did. But you turned it down?" Dylan had no idea why. The role was perfect for her. She'd be in the spot light and it'd open up to so much more in the future. Exactly what she had said she wanted.

"I did."

The room was so quiet that you could hear a pin drop. Should he ask why now? Might as well or someone else would. "Can you explain what you didn't like about it?"

"The role was perfect. Everything was."

"So why didn't you take it?" he asked.

"Because it was my dream, but my dream has changed."

Obviously I haven't been listening as good as you think. Because I have no clue what it is. "Then what do you want?"

Her eyes filled with tears again and his heart ached to make it all better for her. Whatever she wanted, the moon, the stars, whatever, he'd get it for her to bring that smile back.

"You."

He blinked. "Me? You have me sweetheart."

"No. Not like I want. If I left, I'd be working endless hours on a set, and in different country. I wouldn't be coming home to you. My dream is to wake in the morning and make you breakfast and at night after dinner, snuggle up on the couch and watch a movie, or read a book. I was chasing what I thought I wanted, but found something so much better. No spotlight could ever compete with the quiet nights we have alone. I wouldn't trade them for anything."

"You mean you want to stay here, with me?"

"It's where my heart is Dylan. I love you and I can't picture my life without you in it."

The room said "awe" in unison. Dylan didn't care. To him, it was just him and Sofia standing there.

"Sofia, I love you so much. I never thought I'd be able to say those three words, but with you, everything somehow is...easy. You're the one who makes this place a home. Without you in it, it'd be just stuff I don't care about. I was willing to let you go, but I have to admit, nothing makes me happier than knowing you want to stay."

She smiled up at him. "By your side is where my home is Dylan."

He said, "Right now I regret only one thing."

"What is that?" she asked.

"Inviting all these people over." She smiled and he looked around the room. What better time than now? Everyone she loved was present. He said, "Stay here for one second. Don't move."

"Okay."

Dylan walked over to Filippo and whispered in his ear. He nodded and Dylan returned to Sofia's side.

"Sorry, I needed to take care of something."

"With my father?"

"Yes. Now where were we?"

"I think we agreed I'd stay," she said.

"No. I think I was telling you how much I love you."

She smiled. "I'll never get tired of hearing you say that."

"Good, because I asked all these people over to celebrate some big news. I don't think we should disappoint them."

"So you *want* me to take the job?" Sofia asked looking puzzled.

"No. I think we should make this an engagement party." Dylan dropped down on one knee. Once again the room buzzed with excitement. Maria hushed them all. "Sofia, I don't have a ring to put on this lovely hand of yours, but what I can give you is my heart. I love you and you'd make me the happiest man alive if you'd do me that honor of being my wife."

Sofia burst into tears and shouted, "Yes! Yes! It's all I want because you already have my heart too."

Dylan stood up and leaned down and kissed her. Not the way he wanted, but one that would show her, how much he loved her. Once again he felt her sway a bit. "Are you sure you're okay?"

"Yes. Like you said, it's been a crazy day. But ending on a perfect note."

Maria came over and looked at Sofia closely. "Are you?"

Sofia shook her head. "No. I went to the doctor today and they said no."

"You were at the doctor today? Is everything okay?" Dylan asked.

"Yes, the doctor said it was just stress."

Fuck. And I did all this? "I'm sorry sweetheart. I didn't know. I never would've invited everyone or surprised you if I knew. Why don't you sit down and I'll get you something to eat. Maybe put your feet up and I'll"

"Dylan, stop. I'm fine. It's nothing. I'm just tired, but I'm fine," Sofia said.

Maria shook her head. "No you're not stressed, you're having a baby."

Dylan looked down at Sofia who was looking at her mother. Both stunned. Sofia said, "Mama, they did a blood test and said I'm not."

"You can listen to them, or listen to your mother. You know, I'm always right," Maria said.

Rosslyn said, "My money is on Mama."

Dylan wasn't sure who was right. It didn't matter. The only thing he wanted was for Sofia to be well. "Either way, you should be sitting down and resting."

Sofia said, "Dylan, I'm not pregnant."

"Yes you are," Maria said.

Dylan bent over and scooped Sofia into his arms. "Although I appreciate medical science, I've learned a lot over the last few months. First, your mother is never wrong and secondly, you'd make an amazing mother."

Sofia wrapped her arms around his neck and said, "And you a superb father."

Maria exclaimed, "And I'm going to be a Nonna."

The entire room cheered again.

This might not have been anything that Dylan had planned, but somehow it was exactly what he wanted. When

207

the charade was over, he was left with the one thing he couldn't live without. The woman he loves.

He carried her over to the couch and set her down. Her cell phone rang and she pulled it out of her purse.

"It's the hospital," Sofia said showing him the number.

"Answer it. It has to be important." They never would call on a Friday night.

"Hello. Yes this is Sofia. What did you say? Wait a moment could you repeat that?" she pressed the button putting it on speaker phone. "There was a malfunction with the testing equipment. We reran your blood work and it appears that you are pregnant. The test returned positive."

"I'm having a baby," Sofia said.

"Yes ma'am you are. Congratulations."

"Thank you for calling." Sofia ended the call and said, "I guess it's a real good thing I turned down that offer and accepted yours instead."

"You better believe it. Why play a wife and mother in a movie when you can live it right here with someone who loves you?"

"And what's best of all, there's no acting required. I love you Dylan."

"I love you too Sofia." Dylan placed a hand on her stomach and added, "And you too little one."

Dylan was used to getting what he wanted, and his plans never failed. But today, he couldn't be happier that they had because having Sofia by his side, making a family with the woman he loves, that was what he wanted all along. It just took him longer to realize it. But everything was clear now. His dream, no their dreams, were coming true.

The End

When Sparks Fly Series:

Drive Me Wild

Plug Me In

Turn Me On

****

The Blank Check Series:

Book 1: The Billionaire's Rival

Book 2: The Billionaire's Charade

Book 3: The Billionaire's Scandal

Book 4: The Billionaire's Regret

Book 5: The Billionaire's Deception

Book 6: The Billionaire's Revenge

The Billionaire's Rival

Charles Lawson carries the weight of the entire family's future on his shoulders. As CEO of Lawson Steel it is his responsibility to ensure their legacy continued for the next generation. First on his agenda is to clean up loose ends from the past. Doing so is risky and if he fails, the price could be great. It's a risk he's willing to take.

Rosslyn Clark loves her life as is, but family is everything to her. When her parents find themselves in a crisis, all she loves is at risk. Whether she likes it or not, sometimes change is inevitable.

As Charles prepares to seal the deal, he finds one beautiful blonde stands in his way, and things become complicated. Can he continue with his original plan and look at her as collateral damage or has Rosslyn become something more to him?

Rosslyn finds herself caught between two powerful men, one she works for, the other, his rival. Will she do what is expected of her, or will she walk away from everything and follow her heart?

****

Barrington Billionaires Series:

Book 1: One White Lie (FREE!)

Book 2: Table For Two

Book 3: You & Me Make Three

Book 4: Virgin For The Fourth Time

Book 5: His For Five Nights

Book 5.5: New Beginning Holiday Novella

Book 6: After Six

Book 7: Seven Guilty Pleasures

Book 7.5: At the Sight of Holly

Book 8: Eight Reasons Why

Book 9: Nine Rules of Engagement

One White Lie

Brice Henderson traded everything for power and success. His company was closing a deal that would cement his spot at the top. The last thing he needed was a distraction from the past.

Lena Razzi had spent years trying to forget Brice Henderson. When offered the opportunity of a lifetime, would she take the risk even if the price would be another broken heart?

Do you love reading from this world? Continue with Always Mine from my sister, Ruth Cardello, Her series will mirror my time line. It isn't necessary to read hers to enjoy mine, but it sure will enhance the fun!

****

Betting on You Series:

Book 1: The Billionaire's Secret (FREE!)

Book 2: The Billionaire's Masquerade

Book 3: The Billionaire's Longshot

Book 4: The Billionaire's Jackpot

Book 5: All Bets Off

Book 6: A Rose For The Billionaire

Book 7: The Billionaire's Treat Novella

The Billionaire's Secret

Billionaire Jon Vinchi is a man with one passion: work. His friends decide to shake him up by entering him as a prize at a charity event.

Accountant Lizette Burke is dressed to the nines and covering for her boss at a charity event. She's hoping to land a donor for the struggling non-profit agency that employs her.

She never expected to win a date with a billionaire.

He never thought one night could turn his life upside down.

One lie stands between them and their happily ever after. Too bad it's a big one!

****

Southern Spice

Derrick Nash knows the pain of loss. But is he seeking justice or revenge? He doesn't care as long as someone pays the price.

It is Casey Collin's duty at FEMA to help those in need when a natural disaster strikes. After a tornado hits Honeywell, she finds there are more problems than just storm damage. Will she follow company procedures or her heart?

Can Derrick move forward without the answers he's been searching for? Can Casey teach him how to trust again? Or will she need to face the fact that not every story has a happy ending?

****

For Honor

Looking for a new Romantic Intrigue? Then you will love the Turchetta's. You met them in both the Betting On You Series as well as Barrington Billionaires Series. Now it is time for an up close look into their lives.

Rafe Turchetta may have retired from the Air Force, but his life was still dedicated to fighting the injustice of the world. There was one offense that went so wrong, and it will haunt him, as it continues to destroy him on the inside.

Deanna Glenn was being tortured by a tragedy, one that she couldn't share with anyone. Time was running out and she needed the lies to cease before she started to believe them herself.

Healing meant returning to where it all went horribly wrong years ago. For Deanna she needed to take on a new identity. For Rafe, that meant doing whatever he needed to in order to get her to speak the truth.

When danger rears its ugly head will Rafe follow his heart and protect Deanna even if it means never learning the truth? Or will Deanna sacrifice her happiness and expose it all?

Books by Ruth Cardello

ruthcardello.com

Books by Danielle Stewart

authordaniellestewart.com

Do you like sweet romance? You might enjoy Lena Lane

www.lenalanenovels.com

BY JEANNETTE WINTERS & LENA LANE

Muse and Mayhem Series

Book 1: The Write Appeal

Book 2: The Write Bride

Book 3: The Write Connection(2019)

Made in the USA
Monee, IL
26 October 2020